THE BOOKSTORE SERIES

A CRINKLE IN TIME

Part 2

ALICE VL

THE BOOKSTORE SERIES
A Crinkle in Time – Book 2

Alice VL

THE BOOKSTORE SERIES
A Crinkle in Time – Book 2

Copyright 2018

Alice VL's The Bookstore Series

Book 2 – A Crinkle In Time

Alice VL

THE BOOKSTORE SERIES
A Crinkle in Time – Book 2

Alice VL

THE BOOKSTORE SERIES
A Crinkle in Time – Book 2

"For one moment in time, for one call of the heart and the mind to the soul, time is nothing. When the soul agrees that there might have been a fault in the stars, the heart, the mind and the soul will come together, and alter one moment in time." – Adelaine Alandrali

Alice VL

THE BOOKSTORE SERIES
A Crinkle in Time – Book 2

Alice VL

THE BOOKSTORE SERIES
A Crinkle in Time – Book 2

TABLE OF CONTENTS

THE BOOKSTORE SERIES
A Crinkle in Time – Book 2

Alice VL

PART ONE

She mustered up all the strength she had left inside of her to turn onto her side, and pull her legs up against her, until her knees touched the warmth of her chin.

She was crippled by fear as she stared apprehensively out in front of her. Her frightened eyes searched for a shadow that had cruelly infested her home, and infected her life only a few minutes earlier.

She could hear the echo of his footsteps as though he was trampling holes through her floor, with each angry step he took. She listened closely as she held her breath to what sounded like a zipper being pulled up.

Holly folded her arms around her belly, and was at once unnervingly aware of a warmth that had begun to seep through her hands. As she lay desperate to identify the warm wetness that was flowing through her fingers, she suddenly heard the slamming of what she was sure was her front door.

Alice VL

THE BOOKSTORE SERIES

A Crinkle in Time – Book 2

The violent way in which a door had been battered and shut echoed down the hall, and right into her bedroom where she was laying motionlessly on the floor, submerged in a pool of her own blood.

She fought desperately to keep her eyes open as they grew heftier with each passing moment, and with each breath she struggled to take. As her tears slowly dribbled from her eyes, Holly laid on her bedroom floor, unable to make a sound and powerless to move. As her blood cascaded around her, the stench in the air began to sicken her. Her body contorted violently when she detected the continuous flow of her own blood all around her.

She could not bear the horrific smell that had begun to immensely frighten and terrorize her. The whiff of death wholly plunged her into a kind of stench she had never inhaled or smelled before.

The waves of panic that had begun to overwhelm her, sent a panic-filled shudder down her spine. She was suddenly cold and sleepy. She moved her toes slightly, and was at once aware of a throbbing, burning sensation in her legs that travelled right down to her feet and into the very tips of her toes.

THE BOOKSTORE SERIES

A Crinkle in Time – Book 2

The warmth that had seeped out below her and soaked into her body, had become ice-cold. She was once again gravely aware of how distressingly weighty and sluggish her eyes had become.

The intense discomfort throughout her body became almost too much to endure when she could not determine precisely where her soreness was coming from. She could not identify a single segment of her body that was not aching. She wanted to surrender to the pain; to break down and scream out in agony, but even that seemed almost too excruciating to do.

Her breathing had become severely labored, as she distraughtly gasped for air to fill her lungs. With each breath she fought to take, she was sure that her airways were severely restricting her ability to breath, and that her lungs could no longer take in even a single breath of fresh air.

Her legs were cold and shaking irrepressibly. Holly realized in horror that she was completely naked from the waist down. Again, she tried to move, but she could barely move a finger, or lift an arm.

With every bit of strength left inside of her, she turned onto her back, and stared up at the ceiling, still frantic not to surrender to the darkness that was threatening to overpower her. She turned her head, and stared at the calendar that she had hung up behind her bedroom door only a few weeks earlier.

"February 12th, 2005 …"

She whispered huskily and knew instinctively that it would be the date permanently marked and inscribed on her tombstone.

'How often didn't I reach this day in all the years I have lived, and I never knew, I never knew …' She thought sadly as she lay staring at the date. Her eyes moved forward two days when she noticed the enormous red circle she drew around the 14th, "Valentine's day …" She whispered softly before she slowly turned away from the calendar, and allowed her eyes to rest on the ceiling once again.

She felt a sharp twinge come from her belly. When she could no longer control her agony; when the fear began to cripple and wholly engulf her, she finally cried out in grueling pain when she realized that the warmth was nothing more than her own blood that was seeping from her stomach. She had only moments before, been gutted with her own kitchen knife, and left for dead by a man she had known for most of her adulthood.

Adam Weston had relentlessly pursued her during her years at college, and when she fell in love with his best friend, Mark Quinn, Adam slowly withdrew from their crowd as a way to punish her.

When he later joined Mark as a firefighter in Hazel Creek, Holly was sure that Adam had finally come to terms with her relationship with Mark, and that he had ultimately moved past his utter sensitivity of that, that immensely plagued him; the fact that Holly had rejected his advances.

Adam was assigned to District 61, while Mark was stationed at District 59 shortly after they had completed their training in Queenstown. When they both were sent to the city to complete the arduous training that would later make firemen out of them, their friendship once again became more like a brotherhood.

Holly was pleased and relieved that they were able to reconnect and place their differences aside. In no way at all, was it her intention to dissolve a friendship that had been around long before Holly showed up.

After Mark and Holly's wedding in September the previous year, Holly couldn't help but notice a restlessness about

Adam, almost like some sort of turmoil that was brewing inside of him.

She felt incredibly awkward around Adam, and she became intensely suspicious of him when he would show up at their apartment unannounced, especially when Mark was on shift. He would frequently show up as an uninvited guest, and falsely claim that he was simply there, waiting for Mark to end his shift and meet up with him.

Holly would feel increasingly compromised when he would stand particularly close to her, and when he tried to kiss her once, she insisted that he no longer show up at their apartment while Mark was at work. Holly in no way at all, ever mentioned her feelings of discomfort around Adam to Mark, and she did not have the heart to tell Mark about Adam's intrusiveness towards her.

Holly and Mark had moved into their apartment shortly before their wedding a few months ago. They had met when Holly began her first year at college in Hazel Creek. She had only months before enrolled in a graphics design course, while Mark was keen to complete a certified paramedic's course with Adam.

Adam and Mark were close friends, a sort of a

brotherhood that Holly could never quite understand, one that dated back to their primary school years. They had met in grade two, and were inseparable almost from day one.

Mark's mother, Shirley would often tell Holly stories of how the two boys would spell nothing more than utter trouble together. They were persistently up to no good, but Arnold, Marks's father would regularly reassure Shirley that they were simply young boys doing what boys did best, cause havoc.

Yet, Shirley couldn't shake a feeling of uneasiness and anxiety around Adam. She once told Holly how Mark would appear to be disciplined, well-spoken and well-mannered when Adam wasn't around, but the moment that Adam showed up, Mark's attitude would be altered at once.

When Sarah met Adam, she had no desire at all to become romantically involved with him, but they became friends all the same. Adam seemed rather odd looking to Holly, and from the very beginning, there was something that unnerved her about him.

He had a way of peering over his glasses at Holly, which would leave her feeling as though he could see right into her soul and below the depths of her skin. She would often catch a glimpse of his eyes trailing over body, and she would at once fold her arms around her, desperate to shield her body from his piercing glare.

The way he looked at her would leave her feeling as though he was undressing her with his eyes and with his mind. One more occasions than one, Holly would walk away from him feeling naked, violated and disgusted. Adam made no excuses for his behavior, and when Holly once asked him why he would stare so piercingly at her, he simply laughed it off.

"I don't even realize I'm staring, Holly. Are you sure I do?"

"Yes Adam, and it makes me uncomfortable. I don't like it." She would snap at him before she would walk away and avoid him at every corner and turn for the next couple of days.

His sandy blonde hair seemed unruly and unwashed most of the time, but his darker than midnight eyes sent tremors down her spine each time she would look into them. Holly could not help but often think that no-one, but his mother could consider Adam worthy of love and care.

Adam was self-centered, egotistical and dark. There was a darkness about him that would frighten Holly immensely. She would catch glimpses of his facial expressions as they drove past an accident scene, and by the unnerving smile on his face, Holly knew that Adam's behavior was not normal. It was almost as though he was relishing in the horror, and that his eyes were feasting on the sight of blood.

Often, she would hear him tell Mark about an animal that he found in the middle of the road after it was struck by a car. The way in which he described the brutality of the accident and the subsequent injuries, left Holly reeling.

She by no means at all, found him attractive in any way. He had filled out rather early on, but his cheek bones gave him a skeletal look. It was clear to Holly that his muscled look was as a result of hours in the gym, and endless skiing holidays throughout the years.

He was by no means at all a good-looking man, but his physical appearance made him attractive to the opposite sex, or so it seemed to Holly. He took great pride in his body, and again, Holly couldn't help but wonder if he was trying to overcompensate for his lack of manly beauty.

When Holly met Mark, she was at once bowled over by his warm and energetic nature. She was instantly mesmerized by his forest green eyes. When she looked into them for the very first time, she was reminded of ripples in a pond. It would tell her of a forest quenched after it rains, and it would reflect the ocean's temperament during a storm.

His eyes were almost as though there was a promise that spring was about to push its way through piles and piles of snow after an especially cold winter. She fell hopelessly in love with his dark, not quite black hair.

She adored the way the fragments of color seemed as though it had bled out like ink hemorrhaging from a pen, and replaced by tones of grey almost as though they were apologizing to him. Mark was the kind of man that stopped her in her tracks.

The way in which his weak smile and nonchalant gaze caught her attention, reinforced the fact that Mark had no idea how strikingly attractive he was. What appealed to her the most was how modest he was, and how his blush was a dead give-away to his bashful nature.

He was as handsome as they come, but it could in no way at all, compare with his beautiful nature. He would speak slowly and softly. Holly could barely remember a single day that Mark raised his voice at her.

She often told him that he could just as well be the honey

pot that attracted the bees. Strangers would warm up to him instantly, while old friends would stand protectively beside him. He couldn't hurt a fly, and not once did Holly ever see him lose his temper or act on impulse or frustration.

He was everything Adam was not and again, Holly could not quite uncover the secret to their rock-solid, and loyal friendship. It almost did not seem natural to Holly. She was certain that she often caught glimpses of agitation from Mark following a frustrating conversation with Adam. There were times when Holly could swear that Mark felt the need to force tolerance for Adam.

Holly Mackenzie was born in Hazel Creek, and was raised by her devoted mother after her father passed away only a few months after she was born. Danielle Mackenzie once told her the story of how Holly had inherited her father's appearance, from her pearly blonde hair right through to her hazel eyes. Her emotions were as his, not easily hidden on her innocent face.

When she felt pain, just like Arthur Mackenzie, Holly's was evident in the crease of her brow and the down-curve on her full lips. Danielle often told Holly how she thought her face was cut out right from the pages of a magazine, and shown to God before she was born. She was a beautiful girl who stopped growing before her sixteenth birthday. Holly was not at all beautiful in the way that beauty was measured.

Her skin was not perfect, her hair often too curly, and there was nothing piercing about her eyes. She was shorter that the average woman, yet, it was in her ordinariness that she was extraordinary.

Holly grew up as a simple girl. She was always the one to help those around her, and she was utterly grateful for all she had, and all Danielle was able to give her.

But, Holly had a smile that could catch anyone off-guard, and when she laughed, it was almost as though the entire world would come to an abrupt end, and laugh her laugh with her. Mark once told her that to be around her made him feel as though he was someone important. Regardless of the season, she would project endless summer rays to warm him and rejuvenate his spirit

Holly and Danielle would regularly visit Arthur's grave and religiously place flowers at his tomb stone. It was during one of those visits that Danielle Mackenzie told Holly how her father, Arthur, was killed on a bright, sunny, Sunday morning.

Their morning began just like a hundred Sunday

mornings before that. Yet, Danielle told Holly how something felt different that day. Something felt not quite right, but she just couldn't put her finger on it.

The sunrise was tainted by a pinkish glow, unlike any other Sunday before. When she stood staring out of her bedroom window, she was sure that the clouds were tinted, and that the colors had spread across the sky announcing an unexpected event, as if by a celestial hand.

But, other than any morning before, the air was almost too clear, the morning shadows too distinct, and the water in their pond glittered like she had never seen before.

Arthur was an avid cyclist who took immense pride in his appearance, his fitness and his health. He was habitually complemented on his physique, and Arthur would contribute his energy and well-being to that of years of cycling.

He would cycle each morning before work, but on Sundays, he would sleep in for an extra hour, before he set out and cycled through Hazel Creek, and out on hiking trails for most of the morning.

When Arthur failed to return home around lunch time, Danielle grew worried and could not shake the feeling that Arthur had possibly met some terrible fate. In all the years they had been married, Arthur had never diverted from his course or altered his trail. He had never arrived home late on any given day, and when Danielle waited a half an hour longer, she quickly bundled Holly into her car seat, before she set out on the trail he would religiously follow.

It couldn't have been more than a mile from their home, when Daniella spotted his bicycle peek out from a ditch slightly off the road. She grew overwhelmingly anxious when she pulled up at the scene, and was horrified to find Arthur trapped in a ditch, unconscious and bleeding from a wound on his head.

She was almost hysterical when she tensely flagged down a motorist who dialed for an ambulance as Danielle frantically tried to revive him. It was too late. The coroner estimated his time of death as almost an hour before their arrival, and assured Danielle that she had done all she possibly could, but that there was nothing that could be done for him.

There was evidence that he was involved in a hit and run accident, but they were never able to identify the vehicle responsible. Daniella was shattered by Arthur's sudden and untimely death, and even though he had left them financially well taken care of, she struggled enormously to raise Holly without him.

Danielle adored Holly, and devoted herself to the little girl who would grow up without a farther. She had no desire to bring another man into the home she once shared with Arthur, and she ended up living out the rest of her days fiercely protective of, and dedicated to Holly. As she focused on raising Holly, there just never seemed to be room for anyone else in Danielle's life.

Holly was a short few months away from graduating from college, when she walked into her mother's bedroom early one morning. She found it odd and uncharacteristic of Daniella to sleep in, and when she had not yet made their morning coffee, she went to check in on her mother.

Holly was horrified and in a state of shock to discover Danielle's lifeless body. She was devastated that Danielle had passed away in her sleep during the night, with no prior indication of poor health or any other evidence to indicate that Danielle's life was about to come to an abrupt end.

Holly was equally distressed to learn of the autopsy results, wherein her cause of death was confirmed to have been nothing more than a failing heart. It made no sense to her, and when Holly reflected on the days leading up to her mother's death, there was again, no warning, nothing at all to indicate that Danielle was unwell, or that she would simply go to sleep, and never wake up again.

Holly was convinced that her mother had lived out her days pining for Arthur, and by the time Holly reached the age of twenty-two, she was sure that Danielle had died of a broken heart.

When Holly inherited the home Arthur once bought Danielle, she was too shaken and too emotionally spent to live a day longer in her childhood home without her mother. It was the home her father had proudly presented Danielle with and brought Holly home to.

Overcome by sadness of having lost both her parents, Holly did not hesitate to place their house on the market. Before the first thirty days were over, Claire Swanson had sold the house on behalf of Holly to a young couple about to start their very own family.

Holly used the proceeds of the sale to convert a loft in the apartment Mark had bought only weeks earlier, into a studio where she could work from home. Adam had hinted on numerous occasions that Holly and Mark take him on as a roommate, but Holly would never entertain the idea.

Adam's anger and resentment towards Holly mounted with each passing day, and when Mark wasn't around, he would glare at her with what seemed like pure hatred to Holly. She was convinced that she could see the invisible daggers that his eyes were shooting at her, each time Adam would stare.

THE BOOKSTORE SERIES
A Crinkle in Time – Book 2

Alice VL

PART TWO

While Holly lay gasping for breath in her own pool of blood on her bedroom floor on that wintry Friday night, she reflected on the events of the day. Her mind drifted back to that very morning, before her heart began to hammer ferociously when the news she had heard only that morning, echoed through her mind.

She had been feeling unexpectedly worn-out and inexplicably rundown in the days leading up to that morning. She could barely focus on the book designs she was hired to do, and was sure that she was coming down with the flu.

Holly made an appointment with her general practitioner only the day before, and when Mark left for work that Friday morning, she thought it best to tell him about her appointment after she had seen her doctor.

When she arrived at her doctor's consulting rooms, she was thankful to be showed in at once. She quickly changed into the robe Dr. Burgh had given her, before he asked for a urine sample from her. When she handed the sample to his nurse, she quickly made her way over to be examined.

"So, you're not feeling too well?'

"No, I am so tired, and I've completely lost my appetite."

"Are you sleeping alright?"

"Yes, too much I think? I feel so foggy-brained most of the time."

When he examined her breasts, Holly cringed slightly. "Sorry, it's cold, and sensitive ..." She quickly explained before he continued to examine her.

"I do see a little redness in your throat and ears. You might just have a slight infection following a bout of flu, or perhaps a cold. Often, we don't know we have a cold ..."

"I was feeling a little feverish a few days ago?"

"That could be from the infection ..." He quickly made his way over to his desk, and began writing out a prescription for her.

Holly swiftly changed back into her clothes when his nurse walked back in. Holly made her way back to his desk, and took an empty seat in front of him. When Dr. Burgh read what seemed to be a report, he quickly crumpled up the prescription, "Well, that won't do …" He smiled as he peered over his glasses, "You are going to have a baby, Holly …"

Holly stared at him, unsure of whether she had in fact, heard him accurately the first time. She carefully leaned forward before she whispered, almost as though she was defending her question from the world, "Am I pregnant?"

Dr. Burgh smiled again, and turned the report around for her to see, "You sure are, Holly."

Holly scrutinized the report he was dangling in front of her, but when she could not decipher it, or make head or tail from a single word, she sat back and smiled broadly.

"You are almost nine weeks along. I am going to prescribe you something for that infection. It won't harm the baby, and then, some vitamins to supplement your diet. Come and see me in a month for your first ultra-sound, alright?"

Holly took her bag and got up to leave. She quickly shook his hand, and took the prescription from him,

"Any questions, Holly?"

"No? I mean, not right now …" She began trembling

slightly and realized at that very moment that she had no idea what she was doing. For an instant, she wished she could see her mother just one more time, and tell her that she was about to become a grandmother. She wanted more than anything to have Danielle with her on what felt like a long, lonely and scary road ahead of her.

She had no idea of what to expect, and she was in no way at all, prepared to raise a baby. She had no-one to guide her, and more than anything in the world, she wanted Danielle back.

When the news began to sink in, Holly's initial fears and misgivings turned to absolute ecstasy. Discovering that she was pregnant was unexpected, and not quite the perfect time, but at the same time, she couldn't quite deny the feeling that having a baby at that point in her life, was at precisely the right time.

As she made her way back to her car, she noticed an enormous sign above a bookstore she had never quite spotted before. "Fine Books? Hmm …" She frowned and tried to think how it was possible that she had never seen the bookstore before.

She turned away from her car, and made her way towards Fine Books, the bookstore she had noticed for the very first time right in the center of town. When she walked through the large wooden doors, she was at once intimidated by the chiming of a bell, announcing her presence.

For a moment, she felt as though she was intruding in someone's home, and when she glanced around her, she was pleasantly surprised by the countless books that were displayed on beautiful, hand-carved, wooden shelves.

It was almost as though a Victorian era had escaped the new world as it continued to exist behind those enormous wooden doors, while the rest of the world carried on without appreciating the importance of a beautiful era.

There were roughly a hundred shelves fanning out from the reception area. A handful of people were sitting at tables, working quietly. Rows and rows of neatly organized books with their spines facing outward were lined up with precision. Each book was color coded, and sections were arranged alphabetically.

When Holly glanced over to her right, she noticed a reading lounge with more book shelves, a leather arm chair, a couch, and a dozen floor cushions. There was an enormous coffee table in the center of the lounge, and at least four more strategically placed in each corner of the lounge.

There was a certain stillness that was almost deafening, but the coziness of the rich, burgundy carpet muffled the vibrations that were threatening to break the sounds of silence.

"Good morning ..." Sarah handed Cindy a book when she noticed Holly admiring their bookstore. Holly smiled reservedly when she gazed over the enormous, wooden and hand-carved counter that was richly polished.

"Hi, I've never noticed this place before? It is absolutely beautiful."

"Thank you, we think so too. This is what we call our magic place. We're glad you found us ..." Cindy Swanson smiled when she hurriedly made her way around to where Holly was standing.

"I am Cindy Swanson, and this is my daughter, Sarah Kingsley ..." Sarah smiled as she too, made her way over to where Cindy and Holly were standing.

"My name is Holly, Holly Quinn ..." She shook their hands one by one before she hurriedly glanced around her again, still utterly mesmerized by the beauty of the bookstore.

"I can't believe I've never heard of this place before. It is so beautiful, almost like magic …"

"Thank you, so much. I like the word magic …" Sarah smiled, pleased that a new customer was totally enthralled with Fine Books.

"You will definitely see me around here more often, especially now that …" Holly became bashful when she bowed her head before she hurriedly gazed back at Cindy, "I've just, I've just found out that I am going to have a baby. I haven't told my husband yet. I thought I'd come and have a look at some books. As a first-time mother, I actually have no idea what I'm doing?" She giggled nervously before her voice trailed off when she realized that she had begun rambling.

"Congratulations! For that, you have definitely come to the right place." Cindy placed an arm around Holly's shoulder, before they made their way over to their reading lounge. She quickly showed Holly where she could find the books she might be interested in and invited her to take her time.

When she was satisfied that Holly was comfortable and had found her way around the shelves, she gentle patted her on the back before she made her way back to the counter.

Alice VL

Holly ran her fingers through the spines of books that were neatly stacked against each other. There were hundreds of books that promised to see her through her entire pregnancy, as well as once her baby had come into the world. Holly felt a little panicky when she read title after title.

When she finally settled on what she thought was a beginning, she sat down on the leather arm chair in the corner of the reading lounge. She turned to switch on the lamp when her eyes caught a beautiful, old, leather-bound book that looked to her as though it was at least a hundred years old. She glanced around her and with great care, she picked up the book, and slowly turned the pages. "Passage of Time …" She read out softly as she carried on turning the pages. It suddenly dawned on her that it was a book she had first heard of in another book she had read only a few short months ago. "What was that book?" She whispered softly, trying desperately to fit together the puzzle of the book she was holding in her hands.

"For one moment in time, for one call of the heart and the mind to the soul, time is nothing. When the soul agrees that there might have been a fault in the stars, the heart, the mind and the soul will come together, and alter one moment in time."

Holly gasped for air when she realized she was reading a

paragraph that Sarah Kingsley, then Swanson had written in her own book, 'A Moment in Time.'

She was intrigued, yet, she was hesitant to admit that she had a hard time believing Sarah's accounts. Nevertheless, she was fascinated by the Legend of Adelaine Alandrali, and as enthusiastically as she tried, she could not put the book down even for a moment.

It was almost time to close Fine Books and lock the doors for the evening time when Sarah suddenly realized that Holly had not yet appeared from their reading lounge from the moment she had walked in a few hours ago.

When Cindy said goodbye, Sarah quickly made her way over to Holly. "Is everything alright? Did you find what you were looking for?"

"Yes, thank you." Holly smiled before she peered up at Sarah.

"What have you got there?" Sarah's heart missed a beat and began to race irrepressibly when she documented the book that Holly was holding. She was at once displaced and entirely befuddled as she tried to figure out how Holly could possibly have found Passage of Time.

Holly could at once detect the bewilderment in Sarah's eyes. She closed the book, and promptly turned the cover to Sarah, exposing the title of the book to her.

"Where did you find that book?" Sarah whispered as her heart began to pound wildly once again. Sarah was at once defeated by an eerie sense of dread, one she hadn't felt in years.

"It was laying here, on the coffee table ..."

Sarah hastily took the book from her before she glanced over at the coffee table. She had not removed the book from the shelf in what was once her very own reading corner, a room she had now converted into a study where she sat writing her stories all day long.

Sarah knew that the book was hidden, and for a moment, she wondered if Cindy hadn't perhaps placed the book there by accident. Holly was at once flustered when she noticed that Sarah had unexpectedly turned ashen almost straight away.

When she gazed back at the book in Sarah's hands, she suddenly realized that Sarah's connection with that book was authentic and that perhaps, her story was not at all as preposterous as it once seemed to her. "You are Sarah Swanson, author of A Moment in time?"

Sarah nodded as she clutched her book, afraid of letting it fall from her grasp.

"Wow, I read your book, and I read all about Passage of Time. Is it true?" Holly stood up before she excitedly rushed over to where Sarah was standing. "Is any of it true. The Legend of Adelaine Alandrali? Did you really go back in time?"

Sarah was mortified by Holly's questions, but she smiled politely before she lowered her head, "Yes, it happened exactly as I wrote it, Holly …"

Holly instinctively placed her arms around Sarah, and hugged her tightly, "I am so glad you got your one more last chance, Sarah. I can't imagine the pain you went through."

Sarah smiled at Holly, whose tears had begun to shimmer in her eyes, "I am too. That book found me somehow, and gifted me with a little bit of its magic."

Holly turned around and hurriedly grabbed the stack of books she had piled up on the coffee table, "I better be off. I want to surprise my husband Mark tonight with the news, and make him something special for supper. I'll just take these for now." Holly handed Sarah the books and followed her as they made their way over to the counter.

Alice VL

"Please come back any time, Holly. For any reason, for anything at all, you come back here when you need to." Sarah smiled when she handed Holly her books. She was instantaneously and intensely aware of a familiar sense that somehow, that book did not show up for no reason, or by chance.

She was terrified that it might involve Holly, and she wanted her to know that she could return to Fine Books whenever she needed to.

"Oh, you'll definitely see me here again! Good luck, Sarah, and I look forward to your next book."

"Thank you so much, Holly. I appreciate it, and good luck to you too. Be careful ..."

Holly hurriedly left through the same doors she had come in, and when she heard the bell chime, she was at once reminded of how Sarah depicted the chiming doorbell when Daniel showed up at the bookstore one night.

As she hurried out to her car, Holly quickly glanced at her watch, "It's getting late, I must hurry. I hope Mark isn't working late tonight?" She placed the books on the passenger seat, before she hurriedly drove off, and back to their apartment.

Before Sarah locked up for the night, she hastily ran up the stairs and into her study. She anxiously placed Passage of Time back on her shelf, where she had kept it safely hidden from the world. She could by no means at all, shake the feeling that something was wide off the mark with Holly, and she could not deny a feeling of uneasiness that had begun to engulf her.

As she stood staring at her book that had so magically appeared on a coffee table in the reading lounge, Sarah urgently dialed Cindy on her mobile phone.

Sarah was at once relieved when Cindy answered after the first ring, "Hello?"

"Hi mommy …"

"Sè? What's the matter?"

"Nothing. It's just, did you have Passage of Time in the reading lounge today?"

Cindy paused for a moment as she replayed the events of that day, "No? I haven't taken that book out since, well, you know?"

Sarah frowned again and could not ignore the sudden battering in her chest as panic entirely consumed her. It was only her and Cindy in the bookstore, and except for their cleaning lady, Martha, there was no-one else who had access to the book.

"I don't think it was Martha?" Sarah whispered croakily, desperate for an explanation.

Cindy could detect the utter confusion, paired with devastation in her voice, and became suspicious almost straight away, "I don't think so, baby? But maybe she was dusting the shelves and thought it should be in the reading lounge?"

"Yeah, it could be. I just, I have a bad feeling, mommy?"

"What about, Sè?"

"I don't know? I'm not sure. Maybe about Holly? I found her reading the book, and she said she found it on the coffee table?"

"Oh honey, nothing's going to happen to Holly. It was pure coincidence that the book landed up in the reading lounge. Speak to Martha tomorrow, okay? Now set your mind at ease, I am sure there is a perfectly good explanation for this."

"Alright mom, see you tomorrow."

"Sleep well, baby. Megan has just stopped by to pick up

the kids. See you tomorrow ..."

When Sarah ended the call to Cindy, she made a mental note to speak to Martha first thing in the morning. She was determined to make Martha understand that she was never to remove Passage of Time, or any other book from her study. While locking the big, wooden doors to Fine Books, she still could not shake the feeling that Passage of Time had in fact, chosen Holly, and for some reason, Holly would be given one more last chance.

She wanted to reach out to her and warn her, but she had no idea of what to say to her, or how to tell her that something horrific was about to happen. Even as she replayed the scenarios over and over in her head, she could not deny how utterly foolish and insane she would sound to a total stranger she had met only hours before. As with Holly, Sarah could not even begin to imagine the brutal and sadistic way in which Holly was about to meet her fate.

Alice VL

When Holly reached their apartment, she quickly hid the books in her closet. The same books she had bought home with her, before she excitedly dialed Mark's number.

"Hello beautiful?" Mark was happy to hear Holly's voice for the first time since he had left for work early that morning,

"Hello handsome …" Her heart would flutter almost as though a dozen butterflies had entered her, each time he referred to her as beautiful.

"What's up?"

"Nothing much. Are you working late tonight?"

Mark had been working double shifts for the last few months. Not only were they understaffed in all the districts across Hazel Creek, but he welcomed the extra money he earned working double shifts. "Yep. District 61 is short-staffed, apparently, Adam had called in sick, so I'll be standing in until around two in the morning."

"Can't you just come home early just this one night? Is there no-one else you can ask to stand in for him? You've been at work all day, and you've been pulling double shifts for months. Just tonight?"

"I can't, Holly, it's too late to try and find someone to fill in for Adam now. I told my Captain I would. You should have asked earlier. I might still have been able to sort something else out."

"I know. Please wake me when you get home. I want to have dinner with you when you get home."

"Is everything alright?" Mark felt sudden panic make its way into his entire being when he detected the unanticipated urgency in Holly's voice.

"Everything's fine, nothing's wrong. I just see so little of you. We've hardly had a decent conversation in a while. Just wake me when you get home, okay?"

"Alright, see you later, angel. I love you ..."

Holly was disappointed that Mark would be working late again, but when she heard him call her angel, there was nothing else in the world that mattered to her at that very moment. He loved her, and she could not ask for anything more than a man who worked his fingers to the bone for her. "I love you. Be careful out there for me, okay?"

Holly spent the remainder of the evening preparing

Alice VL

supper, cleaning up and putting a load of laundry into the washer. She poured herself a cup of tea before she made herself comfortable in Mark's living room chair. When she turned on the television, she had barely turned to a channel, when she heard an urgent knock on their front door.

Holly glanced down at her wrist watch, and when she realized it was almost midnight, she was at once confused by who it could have been. She was unpredictably panic-stricken and thought that perhaps, Mark might have been injured at work, or worse.

She got up slowly as her heart began to thump irregularly in her chest. When there was a second loud knock, she walked over to the front door as though in a wandering daze.

She hesitated for just a moment before she opened the door. When she saw him standing there, she could at once smell the alcohol on Adam's breath. Holly could barely think of a day that he had been sober lately.

He got through his days drunk, and on the rare occasion, sobered up enough for work. He would call in sick more frequently lately, and both Mark and Holly knew that his growing dependency and secret addition to alcohol was beginning to hinder his ability to work.

Yet, Adam would never admit that he was reliant on liquor and would laugh it off when Mark would try and address it as a problem. He would irately assure Mark that he could quit anytime he wanted to. "Is Mark home?"

Holly was at once irritated by the intrusion while Mark was filling in for him, too drunk to work his shift at District 61

"No. And you'd know that, because you should be at work. Mark has had to do an extra shift because your house is understaffed! Have you no shame, Adam? Mark has been working extra shifts for months, and the one night I wanted him to come home, he couldn't because you called in sick!" Holly was unexpectedly startled by how angry she had become.

"Yeah, yeah ... whatever ..." He pushed past her, staggered down the corridor and into the kitchen.

"Excuse me, Adam? I did not invite you in! I don't want you here when Mark isn't here!" She slammed the front door closed, and tempestuously, followed him into her kitchen hoping that he would leave at once.

"Since when do I need an invitation?"

Alice VL

"Since always, Adam. Mark isn't here, and I think it's inappropriate for you to come by when he's at work, especially when you know he's at work."

"Oh, get over yourself, Sarah! I had no clue Mark was going to fill in for me?"

"Who else? Mark always volunteers for you! He always cleans up your mess, Adam!" She raised her voice heatedly as she desperately tried to swallow her retort. She clenched her fists and gritted her teeth, determined to remain silent, or at the very least, polite. She could feel the blood rush to her face like an acid burning away at her as she fiercely attempted to suppress her rage.

Adam lost his balance at least twice when he walked over to her. He lifted her chin with his one hand, and ran his fingers down her blouse with the other,

"Stop that!" Holly pushed his hands away, and retreated slightly.

She was in no way at all, prepared for a confrontation with Adam, and for the first time since she had met him, she was overcome by an indiscreet fear she had never known before.

When she looked into his eyes, they were narrowed, cold and piercing. There was something in Adam's eyes she had never seen before, and it scared her almost to death. Her heart began to hammer erratically when she realized that she had come face to face with her enemy, one she had not anticipated.

There was a deadness, a kind of a stillness that had replaced the white of his eyes. There was nothing in his eyes that cautioned or alerted her to what was rushing through his mind, but when she noticed his clenched jaw, she knew she was in trouble.

"Stop what? You were a slut in college and you are a slut now! You think you are so much better than me, don't you Holly?" His voice was filled with emotion and raw anger. His unmoving gaze was led by slow, robotic breathing sounds. When he grabbed her hands, she realized how vulnerable and indignant she had become.

"You are hurting me, Adam!"

"Don't fight it, Holly ..."

It was as though Adam had turned into a wild animal. His chest muscles were bulging as he dragged her into her bedroom, and heaved her onto the floor. With the force he sent her down with, she knocked her head on the cold tiles, causing her to lose consciousness almost at once.

When Holly opened her lethargic eyes, she could barely breath, and when her eyes were finally fully opened, she realized that Adam was on top of her. She could smell his sweat, and she could smell the stale smell of alcohol hanging in the air.

Her heart rate accelerated uncontrollably, and when she tried to control her breathing, she realized that he had penetrated her. "I am pregnant, Adam!"

Adam stared at her for a moment, before he carried on thrusting himself into her, "Yeah, right!"

A sudden gush of pain jolted throughout her body. As she tried to fight back, her arms losing tension, and her legs beginning to weaken. She began hitting and punching him with all her might, but it hardly made him flinch. She grabbed at his hair and when he looked at her, she began gouging at his eyes.

This enraged Adam even more, and when he grabbed her hands with one hand, he landed a perfect blow to her face with the other. For the second time that night, Holly closed her eyes, and slipped into a darkness she had never known before.

When she opened her eyes again, Adam was nowhere to be seen. Holly hurriedly rose to her feet, and ran out into the living room. She had no sooner reached for her mobile phone, when Adam came out of nowhere, and completely blindsided her when he grabbed her by her hair.

While dragging her back into her bedroom, Holly noticed blood trickling down her legs. Her stomach tightened, and all she could think of was how Adam had thrust her into a cell of utter fear and total bewilderment. There was nothing in the world that could be more brutal to Holly, than the fact that Adam had brutally stolen their child from them.

"You are going to jail for this, Adam!"

Holly's physical pain was at once replaced by what felt to her as a raging sea of anger that was building up inside of her. All she could think of was the tornado Adam had brought with him, and the path of destruction and sorrow he would leave behind.

He shoved her back onto her bedroom floor, and began stabbing her with the same kitchen knife she had used earlier on in the evening. She could feel the iciness of the knife as it met her flesh, and she could barely ignore the sound it made as the blade was twisted into her.

Alice VL

THE BOOKSTORE SERIES
A Crinkle in Time – Book 2

She could feel each muscle contract as each nerve began to twitch. Holly was desperate to defend herself by guarding her body with her hands, but Adam continued to jab at her until she surrendered, collapsed, and laid her head down on her bedroom floor.

Adam glanced around him and became panicky when he noticed the trail of blood on her floor, and blood spatters on her walls. He stared down at her as the blood oozed from almost every opening of her body.

Still holding the knife in his hands, he wiped the blood of the blade against her bed cover, and hurriedly bolted from Holly's bedroom before running out through the front door.

Holly's eyes were barely open. Her eyesight was blurred as her tears began to blind her. When her breaths grew shorter, all she could think of was that there would be no more walks with Mark, not a single birthday to share or even one more dinner together.

She was trapped between the four walls of her bedroom, lingering between life and death as she grew impatient for her one final breath to come. The pain that had flowed through her body like hot lava only seconds ago, had made way for an icy numbness.

The corners of her eyes were filled with blackness as it ruthlessly began to spread, almost like a virus, through the white of her eyes. She could hear herself breath, and was horrified by the ragged, shallow gasps she was taking.

She had just closed her eyes when she heard her front door open one more time. She no longer cared if it was Adam, or if he was coming back to finish her off. She closed her eyes tightly, and was horrified by the thought that Mark would be the one to find her there. The tears began to dribble from her eyes and down her cheeks when she thought about how this would forever change and taint her beloved Mark Quinn.

In the world she was slowly disappearing from, she could hear him calling out to her. His voice seemed far off, almost as an echo in the distance. She smiled while lying there listening to the far-removed sound of his calming voice. When his voice grew louder, Holly realized that she was not dreaming, but that Mark had come home.

'Was it after two in the morning already?' She wondered, unable to lift her arms or open her eyes. The hooded veil of death was hanging over her as she fought desperately to call out to

Mark. Holly felt a warm hand on her cheek, before he lifted her into his arms.

The tears began to gush unapologetically from her eyes, as he frantically called out her name. Mark was horrified to find Holly lying in a pool of her own blood, in what was supposed to be the safety of their home.

With every ounce of strength inside of her, Holly opened her eyes. It took her a few seconds to find his eyes and focus on them before hers would close one final time. The image of him bending over her was blurry, but she could not mistake the deep green of fresh basil looking back at her.

"Holly! Holly!"

She stared at him, as he frantically tugged at a blanket from their bed, and placed it on her open belly wound.

"What happened? Who did this?" Mark yelled out and frantically dialed for an ambulance.

He stuttered when he spoke to the operator at his own fire station, and could barely give out their address. He was immediately relieved that she had recognized him, and when she assured him that an ambulance had been dispatched, he tossed his mobile phone onto the floor.

"Holly, help is on its way. Just please don't close your eyes! Don't leave me?"

His voice was becoming distant again, as the numbness of sleep slowly overpowered her. In desperation, she sucked in another breath of air that felt like coals of fire had landed in her lungs. A misty veil began covering her eyes, and was slowly blinding her.

She could feel the faint beating of her heart against her rib cage slow down and grow weaker with each breath she took. Holly knew that she was dying, and with the last bit of air she could breathe in, she opened her eyes one last time, "I am so sorry ..."

Every idea, each notion and every single event of the day played out in her mind, demanding attention from her as darkness began to ruthlessly seize her.

He sat holding her in his arms and explored every inch of her face. There was no greyness in her skin, there was nothing to indicate that she had left. Bar for the lack of the usual pink on her cheeks, Mark could have sworn she had simply fallen asleep.

Alice VL

His hand reached for hers, and when he clutched it into his, the tears began streaming down his cheeks when he realized how cold and limp it had become. He closed the eyes of the woman who once danced in the rays of sunlight. The mouth that would smile for no reason at all turned blue, and when he bent down to kiss her, he was horrified by how stiff and rigid they felt.

One last time, he placed his hand over her chest, and listened for even a slight flutter in her heart. There was nothing. She was gone.

Alice VL

PART THREE

"Holly! You are going to be late! This is your final semester, and you cannot afford to miss any of your classes! Heavens child! If you could study as diligently as you sleep, you'd be a brain surgeon by now!"

Holly sluggishly opened her eyes, unsure if she was dreaming, or whether she had imagined it all. She sat up slowly, and sleepily glanced around her. Her eye lids were drooping when she suddenly snapped them open as violently as though she had been woken by sirens wailing.

For a fleeting moment, she felt hole again as she took in the morning light that burst through her window. She listened to the birds outside of her window and for an instant, she was entirely disoriented.

Holly was wholly caught off-guard when she noticed the haunting familiarity of her unexpected surroundings. She closed her eyes quickly and rubbed them furiously. She opened her eyes slowly, and blinked a few more times. She held her breath as she

Alice VL

glanced around the bedroom she had last spent a night in a few years before.

She gasped for air as she clutched at her chest when her heart began to race irrepressibly. When she frantically recalled the memory of where she was only the night before, Holly was sure that she was dreaming, and became deathly afraid of being shaken back to reality.

"Where am I?"

"Holly, are you awake?" She again heard the achingly identifiable voice, she had last heard years ago.

She was at once overthrown by confusion, and was again, not quite sure if she was dreaming, or whether she had in fact, heard her mother's pacifying voice. Holly was about to roll out of bed, when Danielle Mackenzie unexpectedly appeared in her doorway. Holly was at once aware of a sudden chill in the air.

When her eyes caught that of her mother's, the vision of the woman she had lost a short while before became slightly out of focus. There was a haunting stillness in the air as Holly sat staring at Danielle who was clutching a dish cloth in her hands. She was wearing the smile Holly could remember so well, but Holly had almost forgotten the kindness in her eyes. Her red lipstick was the perfect shade of berry red, and her platinum hair tied back as she had done each day, every year since Holly was only a little girl. Holly could barely move while gazing sadly at the mother she had lost suddenly only a few short years ago.

She tried to absorb all there was to drink in about Danielle, afraid that she might wake up from her dream, and forget. When Holly thought back to the previous night, she wondered again if she was dreaming, or if she was stuck in some sort of in-between in the afterlife.

"Did you hear me? Why are you looking at me as though you've seen a ghost?" Danielle shook her head when she walked in, and hurriedly picked up Holly's nightgown that she had left lying on the floor.

Holly's eyes followed Danielle mechanically, as she stared at her mother in disbelief. When a frosty shudder ripped through her, almost like a bolt of lightning to kick-start her, she bolted from her bed, and flung her arms around her mother.

She wrapped her arms firmly around Danielle, and she breathed in the comforting scent of the mother she had yearned for so often. "Mommy …" She whispered through the tears that burst through her eyes, and spilled down her face.

Alice VL

Holly didn't care that she could barely control the misery that came in waves where her sobbing made way for short pauses as she gasped for breaths. As she clung to her mother, she too, could not deny the joy that had settle into her entire being, all at the same time.

"Holly? What's the matter?" Danielle was in no way at all, prepared for her daughter's sudden emotional outburst. There was a rawness to Holly's despair as she desperately tried to muffle the sounds of her weeping against Danielle's chest.

"Did you have a nightmare?"

Holly lifted her head, unwilling to let go of Danielle, and with shaking hands, she gazed into her mother's dark, worried eyes. "I, I don't know, mom? I don't know what's going on?"

"Oh honey, you probably just had a nightmare? Come downstairs and have your breakfast …" Danielle gently dabbed at the tears that were witness to her daughter's startling anguish, before she squeezed her shoulder, and turned to leave.

"Wait! Mom?"

"Yes?" Danielle turned around and frowned when she heard the vibration in Holly's voice.

"What year is this?"

Danielle glowered in confusion and was sure that Holly was still completely dazed and totally disorientated, and not quite awake yet.

"It's 2002. You know that?"

"Yeah, I know ... just checking ..." Holly quickly looked away from Danielle's suspicious eyes, before she turned to leave and hurriedly made her way downstairs, and back into the kitchen.

Holly walked up to her closet and recognized the wardrobe of a young student, her wardrobe of a couple of years ago. She chose a comfortable pair of jeans, a warm sweater and grabbed her sneakers before she got dressed and brushed her hair.

When she reached the bathroom, she was unprepared for the reflection that was staring back at her. Holly inspected every inch of her face, and was at once, completely and utterly displaced. All traces of the woman she was only the day before, was gone. Her hair was longer, her eyes brighter and her skin flawless.

"It can't be, first mom, then me ... younger?" She squinted her eyes and frowned all at once, as she desperately attempted a conversation with her reflection in the mirror. "What's going on? Am I really just dreaming?"

After Holly brushed her teeth, she slowly made her way back into her bedroom. She noticed her college book bag on the floor at the end of her bed, and quickly picked it up. Inside, she recognized her text books, notebooks and the usual stationery. She frowned one more time, before she closed her bag and overcome by perplexity, she glanced around her bedroom again.

On the nightstand next to her bed, she saw her mobile phone. She quickly walked over, and hurriedly looked at the screen. When she spotted the date on the home screen, Holly was again convinced that she was dreaming.

She smirked slightly when she thought of how vivid it all felt to her. She was delighted to have a moment more with her mother, even though it was only a fantasy type of a moment.

When she glanced at the date one more time, she was horrified to discover that she was caught up in a dream that might soon turn into a nightmare. It was the very day that her mother would go to sleep just as she had every other night before, only this time, she would never wake up again.

Holly felt an impeding knot in her throat appear out of nowhere when she thought back to the morning she had discovered her mother's lifeless body in her bed. Her eyes were closed, her skin deathly pale, and her lips had already turned blue.

Holly couldn't help but think that had her lips not turned as pale as the blue of glacier melt water, she would appear to simply be asleep. Holly felt cold shivers run down her spine, as fear travelled through her veins.

She unenthusiastically made her way downstairs before she cautiously strolled into the kitchen. Danielle was sipping her coffee at the kitchen table, and when Holly appeared in the doorway, she looked up and smiled at her. "I've poured you a cup of coffee, come sit with me for a while ..."

Holly quickly placed her bag on the floor and found an empty seat next to her mother. Danielle smiled, before she handed Holly her coffee.

"So, mom? I was thinking of taking the day off today?"

Danielle's eyes squinted before an enormous frown

settled in right between her eyes. "Whatever for?"

Even if she was wandering around aimlessly in a dream where she was being forced to replay the events of her mother's death, Holly knew she could not yet tell Danielle that she had found her lifeless body in her bed the very next morning. "I just, I want to spend the day with you. I want us to do something together?" Holly became tearful, and Danielle could not mistake the subtle tremble in her voice.

"Oh Holly, go to your classes. You can't afford to miss a class now. I promise you, when you get home, we can find something to do later this afternoon, okay?"

Holly sighed when she realized that there was no convincing Danielle to allow her a day off. She slowly sipped her coffee as she relived the events of her mother's passing repeatedly,

"Have you had your check-up lately, mom?"

"What check-up?"

"Your doctor's? The one you do every year?"

"Oh, that's only next month, why do you ask?"

Holly bowed her head, unable to look her mother in the eye. "I just, I want you to do it today … will you? For me?"

Danielle grimaced when she once again detected a quiver in her daughter's voice. "It's too late to get an appointment now? I feel fine, honey." Danielle smiled and placed her hand on Holly's forearm, "I am fine, honey …"

"Mommy, I just, I just have a very bad feeling. I don't know how to explain how I feel or what's going on, but I am begging you to just trust me, to just …" Holly was close to tears when she realized how utterly insane she sounded.

"Holly, this is ridiculous. I don't know what is going on with you, but there is nothing wrong with me. Now, drink your coffee and get to class. I will see you this afternoon, and we can go out for an early dinner and a movie. Okay?"

Holly nodded before she placed her empty cup of coffee on the kitchen table, "Unless, you have plans with Mark?"

"No mommy, I don't. Besides, I'd cancel everything for a date with you …" She walked over to her mother, and gently kissed her on the cheek. "I love you, mama …"

Danielle smiled, and could not quite discard the fear that

had slowly made its way into her heart. Her stomach shifted uneasily when she heard the desolation in Holly's voice. "I love you, honey, now go on!"

Holly stood still as she surveyed her mother for what felt like forever, before she finally walked out of the kitchen and out through their front door. When she reached her Jeep, she slid into the driver's seat, and sat staring at their home.

She had valiantly attempted to choke back the tears in front of Danielle, but as she sat watching their home, the tears savagely began to surge from her eyes. She knew she could not tell her mother the truth. She wasn't even sure she knew what was going on around her.

Was it all simply a dream she was not ready to wake up from? Or was she trapped between life and death? Whatever it was, Holly knew that she had to do something to try, at the very least, to prevent her mother from dying the very next day.

Instead of heading out to college, Holly drove into the dead center of town, and was at once relieved to find a parking space right in front of Fine Books.

When she switched off her car, she was certain that if there was anyone in the entire world that could help her, it would be Sarah Kingsley. While sitting in her car rehearsing the conversation she was desperate to have with Sarah, she had no idea of where to start or how to ask for her help.

Holly climbed out her car, and impatiently walked up to the heavy wooden doors of Fine Books. Before she walked in, she stopped and took in a deep breath of fresh air. As though in a daze, she ambled in slowly and nervously, and when she heard the familiar chiming of the doorbell, she was instantly yanked back to reality.

Her heart began to hammer profusely when she saw Sarah behind the counter. She anxiously made her way over to her and was at once relieved that Cindy was nowhere to be seen.

"Hello, can I help you?"

Sarah smiled when she saw Holly walk up to the counter. She was certain that the tired, timid and nervous-looking stranger standing in front of her had never been to Fine Books before, but she couldn't help but wonder where she had met her previously. She seemed familiar to Sarah, but she could not quite place her finger on it.

"Hi, do you remember me?" Holly began to stutter apprehensively as her voice began to tremble. She knew better than to ask, and although she knew that Sarah had never met her before, Holly could distinctly remember meeting her just the day before.

"I'm sorry, I don't mean to sound rude, but should I?" Sarah frowned as she again felt a vague sense of familiarity that had again, washed over her. For the briefest of moments, Sarah recognized something in Holly's eyes, but before she could identify it, it was gone.

"No, I'm sorry. I just thought that you, I was sure we had met before …"

"That's alright. I have quite a common looking face." Sarah chuckled as she tried to make light of Holly's sudden and detectable sense of mortification. "Is there anything I can do for you?" Sarah was perturbed at once when she noticed the hopelessness in Holly's eyes.

"My name is Holly, Holly Mackenzie …" Holly offered her a trembling hand as an introduction.

When Sarah took her hand, she was again, unnerved by a sense of acquaintance, and she was at once entirely distracted by her cold, shuddering hands. "Pleased to meet you, Holly. I am Sarah Kingsley. My mother and I own this bookstore."

"I know, your mom is Cindy, right?"

"That's right." Sarah smiled when she once again realized how popular Cindy was with the community of Hazel Creek.

"Is there any chance, I mean, can I speak to you? Alone somewhere?"

There was no mistaking that Holly's croaky voice began to tremble fiercely, and when Sarah fixed a gaze on her, she was at once troubled when she realized that Holly had turned ashen.

"Is everything alright?" Sarah grew increasingly anxious by Holly's odd behavior.

"No, and I'm not sure anyone will believe me. I don't know who to turn to, Sarah. I need help. I desperately need someone to believe me and I need help, and you, Passage of Time? I thought I was dreaming, and then I thought I was dead, but I am still here, and I am not waking up? I don't know where I am, but more importantly, it's when I am, that is scaring me."

Her voice trailed off when she realized that she was rambling and that she had no inkling of how to tell Sarah that she had died the previous night, and that she had woken up to the day before her mother was to pass away.

Alice VL

THE BOOKSTORE SERIES
A Crinkle in Time – Book 2

Sarah had instantly turned as white as chalk when she heard Holly anxiously explain events like those she herself, had once tried to explain. Holly's anxiety left her reeling, speechless and temporarily incapacitated as she tried to make sense of what Holly was saying.

She stood as still as a statue, but was at once aware that the hair on her arms and at the back of her neck had stood upright. She hurriedly made her way around the counter, and frantically took Holly's hands into hers. "My mother is out for the morning. Let's go into the reading lounge and talk, okay?"

Sarah's own voice had begun to judder slightly when she spotted the tears that began to shimmer in Holly's eyes. She led Holly to an empty couch in the quiet reading lounge, and sat down beside her. Again, she could not shake the feeling that she had met Holly before, but she could not place her in any given surrounding.

Holly bowed her head, before she wiped away the tears that had begun to seep from the corner of her eyes. She swallowed back on a bulging lump in her throat, before she peered back at Sarah. "I know, I just know that I am going to sound crazy, so please, Sarah, if you don't believe me, there is no-one in this world that will. If you don't believe me, I am trapped in a world I just don't understand."

Sarah felt overwhelming distress make its way into the very core of her when she noticed the utter devastation in Holly's voice.

"I was in here, yesterday. I had a doctor's appointment, and I found out that I was pregnant …"

"Oh? Congratulations!" Sarah took her hand and firmly squeezed it.

"Only …" Holly paused to take in a deep breath, "I, it was a few years from now. Yesterday was not yesterday? It was 2005. Yesterday was 2005, Sarah?"

Sarah frowned but at once understood what Holly was saying. She felt an ice-cold shiver run down her spine when Holly revealed the dismal questions in her eyes.

"I was, I was attacked in my home last night, Sarah. I was raped, beaten and stabbed by my husband's best friend. He left me laying in a pool of my own blood, for dead …" She lowered her head when she heard herself speak, almost as though it was someone else's voice. She knew that it all seemed so implausible and preposterous even to her.

"I woke up this morning, here. Back in 2002, to a time when I was in College? I know this sounds so insane! Yesterday, I sat right over there ..." She pointed to a single seater in the corner of the reading lounge, "I came in for a few books on pregnancy and babies, but instead, I sat there and read Passage of Time ..."

"You read Passage of Time?" Sarah's heart began to clobber so lavishly, she could hardly hear the thoughts that were running around in her mind. The very idea that a stranger had found, and read her special and magical book entirely unnerved her.

"It was laying over there ..." Her eyes trailed over to the coffee table, "It just caught my eyes, and I remembered reading A Moment in Time previously, and it referred to that book, and I was curious ..."

"The Passage of Time was on that coffee table?" Sarah frowned again as she tightened her grip on Holly's hands. She knew that The Passage of Time was kept hidden on a shelf in her study, away from the rest of the bookstore, and out of the public's sight.

"Yeah?" Holly became jittery when she detected the anxiety in Sarah's voice.

"Passage of Time found you, Holly. You didn't find it there, it found you …" Sarah whispered as she stared at her hands. "I keep that book hidden away from all the other books. It found you. You're not dreaming, Holly. You were given one more last chance, just like I was. Do you know about the Legend of Adelaine Alandrali?"

"Yes, I read about it in A Moment in Time. And when I read Passage of Time, I, I knew you couldn't have made it up. So now, when, when all this happened, and I woke up here, I thought that, maybe you can help me? I don't know what else to do, Sarah? Yesterday, you said that I could come back anytime and for any reason. I think you knew, the future you knew what was going to happen?"

Sarah took in a deep breath before she placed her hands on Holly's shoulders. "You were given one more last chance, Holly. You were given one chance to alter your fate, and change your destiny. Somewhere, there must have been a fault in the stars. Somehow, they all agreed to give you a do-over."

Holly smiled sadly, "It's just, my mother passes away tonight in her sleep, or in the early hours of tomorrow morning. And, they will say that her heart just failed, but I know Sarah, I know she died from a broken heart. How can I save her?"

Sarah's heart thumped nervously as though it was about to gallop right out of her chest. "You must try, Holly, you must try and save her. Whatever you can do, you must try ..."

"She won't listen to me, and I can't tell her the truth?"

Sarah turned away, and sat in silence while deep in thought.

"We are going out for an early dinner and a movie tonight. I'll try talking to her again?"

Sarah turned back to Holly, and grabbed both her hands, "Take her to the emergency room. Don't tell her anything, just take her!"

As though a light bulb went off in Holly's mind, she smiled broadly before she bolted to her feet. "Oh, Sarah. That is brilliant! Yes, I'll do that! There is no way she can get out of that one!"

Sarah got up from the couch, and smiled, "There's always a way, Holly and you know where to find me if you need me, okay?"

"Thank you, Sarah. I came in here thinking you might think I am a lunatic, and now, for the first time today, I have a little hope. I don't know what I would have done without you!"

Holly hugged her tightly before she bolted from the bookstore.

Sarah at once called Cindy, eager to tell her about the events that had just take place in their bookstore.

"Good morning, my girl …"

"Morning mom …"

For a second, Sarah felt just as unnerved as she assumed Holly felt when she walked in earlier, "Holly Mackenzie was just here …"

"Who?"

"We don't know her mom, yet, but we did three years from now …"

"Yet? You've just met her, haven't you? Three years from now?"

"This is crazy, I hadn't met her until today, but Holly insists we met almost three years from now …"

"You met three years from now, as in past tense? You are making no sense Sarah, and the last time you sounded this crazy was …" Cindy gasped for air when she instinctively understood what Sarah was saying. "Sarah?"

Alice VL

THE BOOKSTORE SERIES
A Crinkle in Time – Book 2

Sarah remained silent, unsure of what to say next.

"Oh no, Sè, what happened?"

"She actually came into Fine Books yesterday, which was in 2005 according to her. She died that night, but to her it was last night, and she woke up this morning, a day before her mother is to pass away." Sarah paused to take in another breath of fresh air as she herself, tried to absorb all she was saying. "She says that when she came in yesterday, three years from now that is, she found Passage of Time in the reading lounge. We would never leave that book laying around, and I just knew, mommy. I just knew ..."

"That book found her, Sè, you know that, right?"

"Yes, I do, and I told her that."

"Oh baby, what she must be feeling right now? The confusion, the disorientation, the hopelessness, is there anything we can do to help?"

"Not right now, mom, but she knows I believe her, she knows my story and she knows where to find me. I just wanted to tell you."

"Are you alright, baby?"

Alice VL

"I am sad that something bad happened, but I am glad she got her one more last chance. I just feel so helpless. I want to help her, but I don't know how?"

"Sarah, things will sort themselves out, just be there for her. I'll see you later, my girl."

"Okay mommy, I love you …" Sarah hurriedly ended the call and was once again keenly aware of the hairs that were beginning to rise in her neck once again.

When Holly reached her car, her phone rang suddenly, "Mark?"

"Hi. Where are you?"

Holly was sure that Mark was aware of her absence from class, and she could not ignore the concern in his voice, "I'm not feeling too well. I am skipping classes today. I just want to stay home …"

"You okay?"

"Yes, I will be …" She whispered, at once deeply thankful that he was not standing in front of her.

"Okay. Adam wants to know if he can join us for the game

tonight?"

"The game?" Holly frowned, and could not for the life of her remember any plans made for any game.

"We have tickets for the College football championships tonight? Did you forget?"

Holly at once recalled the game she had reluctantly attended with both Mark and Adam almost three years before. "Oh right. That game. I can't, I promised my mom a dinner and a movie tonight. You and Adam go, okay?"

She felt a quiver run down her spine when she thought of Adam and the mere mention of his name made her sick to her stomach.

"You sure?"

"Yes. Positive. Have fun and I'll see you tomorrow, okay?"

"Okay. Lovey ..."

Holly ended the call before Mark could finish his sentence. "I can't deal with all of that now. I must, mommy comes first ..." She whispered softly before she slid into the driver's seat, and drove back to the home she had shared with her mother for all her life.

THE BOOKSTORE SERIES
A Crinkle in Time – Book 2

Alice VL

PART FOUR

When Holly walked through the front door, she heard her mother singing in the kitchen. She paused for just a moment, frantic to take in her beautiful voice, afraid that she might never hear it again.

She berated herself for the fact that she never once stopped to listen to her mother as she sang and hummed beautiful hymns she once sang in the choir of their Church. Holly slowly tiptoed into the kitchen, and placed her bag on the kitchen table. Danielle turned around and smiled when she noticed Holly grinning from ear to ear.

"I forgot how beautifully you sing, mom. I never really paid attention. I wish I did ..."

"What are you talking about? You hear me sing all the time?"

Holly gazed over at the oven and was at once excited when she smelled the aroma of her mother's freshly baked bread.

"Aaaah, I have so missed your bread, mommy! Come to think of it, I have missed your home cooked meals so much!" She yelled out in excitement before she walked on over to the oven.

"Don't open it!" Danielle swatted her with the dishcloth before Holly burst out laughing.

"I bake bread every week. I don't know what's wrong with you? Are you suffering from some sort of memory loss? Can only be Mark …" Danielle winked before she took a seat at the kitchen table. "Let me just catch my breath, and I'll make us some tea …"

Holly frowned when she noticed how out of breath her mother was, "I'll make the tea, mom …" Holly walked on over to the kettle, and poured them both a strong cup of tea. When she handed Danielle her cup, Holly took the seat right next to her mother, "I thought we should leave for our date at about four?"

"Perfect. I'll be ready. I am so looking forward to an outing with you …" Danielle smiled while carefully sipping on her tea.

Alice VL

When they pulled out of the driveway a few minutes after their agreed upon time, Holly couldn't help but notice how beautiful her mother was. She had dressed up in a beautiful black pair of trousers that was rounded off by a silky, ivory blouse.

Her hair and make-up were beautifully done, and her nails were polished in exactly the same shade as her lipstick. Holly smiled when she noticed Danielle's pair of shoes, and recognized them as a pair she would wear for special occasions only.

While driving down the streets of Hazel Creek in silence, Holly was keenly aware of how tired and worn her mother appeared to be. She could hardly discard the feeling that her mother was not well, even though she knew that Danielle would never tell her, or even admit to feeling run down.

Holly turned off into Hospital Drive, a few blocks before the restaurant they had agreed to have dinner at. She clenched her jaw, hoping that Danielle wouldn't notice, but she noticed at once.

"You turned off one road too soon?'

"Did I?" Holly had no notion of how to respond, and instead, she stared out straight ahead of her.

"Never mind, you can take the next turn, just past the hospital."

Holly ignored Danielle, and when they reached the entrance to the emergency room, her mother glared incredulously at her, "We're at the emergency room? Is everything alright, Holly?"

Holly remained quiet until she pulled into an empty parking space. She turned off the ignition and turned to face Danielle. "Mommy, please, just do this for me. Please let a doctor check you out. I don't want anything to happen to you ..."

"Holly, are you joking?"

"No mommy, I have such a bad feeling ..."

"Well, that is absurd. I am not going in there!"

Holly burst out crying, and at once, she covered her face with her hands as her tears gushed unforgivingly from her eyes when she caught a slight stiffening on Danielle's face. The horror of losing Danielle the very next day looped around in her mind so overpoweringly that there was no room for anything else.

"Holly?" Danielle placed a protective hand on her shoulder, and was at once acutely sensitive to an angst that had begun to overwhelm her. "You're scaring me …"

Holly quickly wiped the tears that had drenched her face, and took her mother's hands into her tear-soaked hands, "Mommy, I know this is going to sound absolutely ridiculous, so you don't have to tell me that, okay? But, I need you to believe me. I so, so need you to believe me."

"Alright honey, what is it?"

"Yesterday, I, found out that I was pregnant. It's a few years from now, and the first person I wanted to call was you, but I couldn't …"

Danielle felt the hair in her neck rise when she noticed the desperation in Holly's voice.

"I couldn't because, you weren't there. You weren't in my future, and you won't be if you don't walk in there tonight. Something is wrong, mommy. I saw you out of breath today, and I can see how tired you are. Just look at the dark circles around your eyes?"

"What are you talking about, Holly?"

"You died mom. You die tonight, or at least in the early hours of tomorrow morning, but you die in your sleep …"

Alice VL

Danielle immediately freed her hands from Holly's and turned away from her. "I have never heard anything so outrageous in my entire life!" Danielle was irritated and at once, livid by what Holly was telling her.

"If it is so ludicrous, mom, then prove it to me! Let the doctor check you out and tell me that you're fine! You once told me to believe in things like this, why can't you just believe with me?" Holly raised her voice slightly, deathly afraid that she would not be able to save her mother.

She didn't care what her mother was thinking or how utterly deranged she sounded, her only mission that night was to have Danielle examined by a doctor, any doctor on call.

"I came back to this moment in time for a reason, mommy, don't steal that from me. Whether you do or don't believe me, give me my one more last chance! Don't take that away from me!" Holly shouted out through her tears, as Danielle desperately tried to make sense of what she was saying.

"What do you want me to tell them in there, Holly? I feel fine!"

"Just tell them that you have a sharp pain in your chest. It's your heart that fails, mom, it just stops."

Alice VL

Danielle frowned, and lowered her head at once. She remained quiet for what felt like forever, until she reluctantly agreed to Holly's desperate pleas, "Alright. But, if nothing is wrong, I never want to hear crazy talk like this again. Do you understand?"

"Yes, mom … I swear it."

Holly bolted from the car, and rushed around to the passenger side. She opened the door for Danielle, and immediately placed her arms around her mother's neck, "It's going to be okay now, mommy …"

"I know it is, because there is nothing wrong!" Danielle still couldn't discard the agitation that had made its way into her mind.

Holly took her mother's hand, and hurriedly led her into the emergency room. "Remember, mommy, a sharp pain in your chest, okay?"

Danielle nodded irritably as they made their way over to the front desk, and introduced themselves to Betty Muller, as was displayed on her name tag.

"Hi, I am Holly Mackenzie. This is my mother, Danielle.

She has been complaining of a sharp pain in her chest all day ..."

The front nurse smiled sympathetically at Danielle, who still thought it was an entire waste of time. She could barely hide the embarrassment that had settled into the very root of her.

"How old are you, ma'am?"

"I am 52 ..."

"Does this happen often?"

"No, I, this is the first time ..."

Danielle was mortified by having to tell such an utter lie, but she swore to Holly that she would have a doctor look her over; she felt obligated and compelled to go along with the sham.

"She actually is in quite a bit of pain ..." Holly was anxious to have her mother checked out as soon as possible.

"Alright, I'll have an ER nurse show her into the emergency room. Will you fill out the forms while we get your mom settled in?"

"Sure, I'd be glad to." She gazed over at Danielle who had been placed into a wheel chair. By the look on her mother's face, Holly knew that her mother was furious, irritated and humiliated.

When they wheeled her out and through the large double doors that lead into the emergency room, Holly was sure that Danielle would give her a piece of her mind later.

Holly had barely completed the forms and handed in Danielle's medical insurance card, when she hurriedly made her way to the nurse's station at the casualty ward.

"Hi. Danielle Mackenzie?"

"Oh right, she is in ward 155. They have taken her for a ECG. She shouldn't be much longer. You can wait for her in her room …"

Holly let out a sigh of relief when she heard that her mother was being scrutinized from top to bottom. She swiftly made her way into her mother's ward, and placed her handbag on the floor, before she made herself comfortable in the visitor's chair. She had just sat down, when she heard a bleeping sound on her mobile phone.

"Can I see you later?" It was Mark. Holly smiled and felt a flurry in her heart when she saw his name on her phone, 'I can't. At the hospital with mom. Everything is fine, just a routine check-up.'

Alice VL

THE BOOKSTORE SERIES
A Crinkle in Time – Book 2

'You sure? Do you want me to come to the hospital?'

'No. Have fun. All is fine. See you tomorrow.'

Holly quickly shut off her phone and waited for Danielle to be brought back to her room. She must have fallen asleep when she suddenly, and distantly heard her name being called out, "Ms. Mackenzie?"

She opened her eyes and saw a man wearing a white coat standing over her. She was at once wide awake, and quickly glanced over at her mother's empty bed. "Where's my mom?"

She felt panic make its way into the very core of her, and when she got up and stood in front of him, she was sure that she could feel every single pound in her chest as it echoed through her entire body and into her ears.

"I am Dr. Joseph Douglas. I will be your mother's Cardiologist from now on ..."

"Cardiologist? Where is she?"

He took in a deep breath and placed his arms on her shoulders when he noticed the fear in Holly's eyes, "We've admitted her to the ICU. The ECG scan shows that your mother is suffering from congestive heart failure."

"Is she going to be okay?"

"We have started her on treatment. She is in the best of hands. It's a good thing you brought her in when you did, tomorrow might have been too late."

Holly burst out crying when she heard Dr. Douglas explain the severity of her mother's condition. All of which, she already knew and had already lived, but had hoped with all her heart she could prevent.

"I am just surprised that she complained of pain. It normally goes undetected. The main symptoms are generally dizziness, fatigue and weakness. She probably just suffered a bout of indigestion, but you did the right thing. Would you like to see her?"

Holly nodded and quickly dabbed at her tears before she picked up her bag. When she reached the ICU, she was at once overwhelmed by the vision before her. Danielle was sleeping in a bed, surround by what seemed as though she was connected to a dozen life-saving and horrendously bleeping machines.

She quietly walked in and placed her bag on the visitor's chair. She leaned over to kiss her mother on the forehead, and again, she struggled to hold back her tears.

Alice VL

"Hey honey ..."

Holly could hear the grogginess and fear in her mother's voice, "Are you okay, mommy?"

Danielle winked and smiled struggling to overcome the sudden exhaustion that had wholly paralyzed her. "You were right, my love. You were right ..." Danielle whispered blandly, her own tears threatening to spill from her eyes.

"Let's not talk about that, mommy. We got here in time and you are going to be just fine. Get some rest, okay. Dr. Douglas knows what he's doing, they've started you on treatment, so everything is going to be okay now. It has to be."

Danielle nodded before she closed her eyes and drifted off to sleep. When a nurse came in to check on Danielle almost an hour later, she at once felt immense pity for Holly.

"Go home and go get some sleep. Have a shower tomorrow morning, and come back and see your mother. She will be fine, you are no good to her here. Dr. Douglas has given her something to relax her and help her sleep. She'll be out for at least ten hours."

Holly reluctantly agreed, and before she picked up her

bag, she kissed her mother one more time, "I love you, mommy ... see you tomorrow. Sleep tight."

When she reached the doorway, she couldn't shake the feeling that she might never see her mother again. She wanted to stay, and hold Danielle's hand all night long. She wanted to sit at her bedside, and talk to her until the sun came up. Holly was terrified that by the time the morning sun shone through, Danielle might be gone from her.

She at once shrugged off all feelings of uneasiness and re-assured herself that they were in time. She had conquered a crinkle in time that had once, shattered her heart. She was in time.

When Holly arrived home, she made her way straight into her mother's bedroom. She put her mobile phone on charge and climbed into her mother's bed, without changing her clothes.

She laid staring at the ceiling, and thought back to the events of the evening. It was her crinkle in time, and she had tricked the stars out of a gut-wrenching fault they were once responsible for.

As she lay quietly in the darkness of the night, she breathed in Danielle's familiar and comforting aroma, before she fell asleep, while reassuring herself again that they were both in time.

Holly was awakened by the ringing of her mobile phone. She glanced over at Danielle's bedside clock, and frowned when she noticed that it was a little after three in the morning. Holly was at once agitated, and was sure that it was Mark calling her, after a few beers with Adam.

She reached for her mobile and was at once unprepared for the number that had shown up on the screen. "This is Holly?"

"Ms. Mackenzie, this is Dr. Douglas from Hazel Creek Medical Centre." He paused for just a moment, "It's about your mother …"

Holly's heart suddenly began to drum violently in her throat. She could hardly breath. It felt as though someone had begun choking her. Her heart was racing at the speed of a jet plane, and all she wanted to do was slam down the phone before he could say anything further. When her entire body erupted into a violent shudder, she remained eerily silent.

"She, she didn't make it …"

Shivers ran down her spine and through her entire body.

Alice VL

Her hands were shaking so fiercely, that she almost dropped her mobile phone. She sat motionlessly as she replayed what he had told her over and over again. She had felt this way once before, only this time, the shock was a thousand times worse.

They were on time. She felt the world slowly disappearing from her as if she was fading away into a darkness she had never known before. She felt numb, and she felt dead inside.

It was only the burning of her lungs and her heart slamming at her chest with such immense force, that she knew she was alive. Her mind was engulfed in a blackness that spread out deep into her soul as it swallowed all her hopes and her dreams. There was a nothingness inside of her that began to savagely taunt her, and nothing made sense to her anymore.

"Could you get someone to bring you to the hospital?"

Holly ended the call at once, and immediately bolted from her mother's bed. She grabbed her bag, and ran out through the front door, still dressed in the clothes she had worn the previous night.

By the time she reached the hospital, she had no memory of getting into the driver's seat or how she had reached the hospital. Running through the huge glass doors of the emergency room, she made her way up the stairs to the fifth floor. When she reached the nurse's station, Dr. Douglas was waiting for her.

She glanced over at the room she had left her mother in only hours before, and was devastated to discover that her bed was empty, and neatly made up, as though she was never there. As though she did not breathe out her last breath in that cold room that was suddenly, filled with death.

She felt her legs grow weak underneath her as she slowly collapsed to the floor. She was overwhelmed by a tormenting pain that had slowly begun to fully submerge her. "We were in time! We were in time!" She shouted out to Dr. Douglas as her tears spilled recklessly from her eyes, "It was all for nothing!" She shouted out again when Dr. Douglas knelt in front of her.

"We did all we could do, Holly. If you brought her in a month ago, it still would have happened. She didn't suffer, I swear it. It was just how it was going to end."

"I don't want to hear it! We were in time! Why did I come back? Why did I come back if I couldn't save her?"

She was making no sense to Dr. Douglas or the nurses that were helping her to her feet. "These things happen, Holly. Her heart just stopped beating ..."

"Why did you let me go home? Why did you tell me she was going to be alright?" Holly shouted out at the nurse who had sent her home only hours before. The nurse turned away from her, and quickly found her way back to the nurse's station.

"It's nobody's fault, Holly, no-one could know?"

Holly leaned in to him, and poked her finger at his chest, "I knew! I knew! I had one more last chance!"

He placed his arms around her and left her to sob in his chest. She buried her head in his white coat and wept hysterically. When she managed to take in a deep breath, she retreated slightly, "Can I see her?"

He nodded and led her down the hall, to a room right at the end of the corridor. Holly gasped for air and stood as though frozen in time when she saw her lying on a cold, white, concrete slab. She was covered by a white sheet, and when Holly walked in, she couldn't help but notice how tiny her mother seemed under that sheet.

Dr. Douglas stood outside and watched her through the glass division. He was saddened by Holly's pain, and he scolded himself for not preparing her for the worst.

Holly lifted the sheet from her mother's face, and rested her head in Danielle's neck, "I failed you, mommy. I knew, and I failed you …" Holly whispered as she clung to her mother's lifeless body. "I don't understand?" She held onto her mother, and when the reality of her passing finally set in, her shock made way for devastating agony and torment.

She stood at her mother's side and sobbed unrestrainedly. Dr. Douglas joined Holly, and quickly pulled the sheet up to cover Danielle's face.

"Can I offer you bereavement counselling, Holly? We have a wonderful team right here that can help you with anything you need?"

Holly shook her head and hurriedly made her way back into the passage, "No. I want, I want to get in touch with the funeral home …"

Holly turned away from him, and as though she was moving on auto-pilot, she reached the elevator and left the hospital without her beloved mother. It all seemed so unreal to her, almost as though it was a movie that was playing out right in front of her.

THE BOOKSTORE SERIES
A Crinkle in Time – Book 2

She was sure that Danielle would walk out of that hospital, and live to meet her grandchildren someday. In no way at all, was Holly prepared to say goodbye to her mother for a second time in her life.

It was just after five in the morning, and instead of heading back home, Holly drove back into town and parked her car right in front of Fine Books. She stared at her mobile phone and wondered if she should call Mark.

She decided to wait until after she had seen Sarah, and as she sat waiting for Fine Books to open, Holly rested her head on the steering wheel, and sobbed until she fell asleep on her arms.

THE BOOKSTORE SERIES
A Crinkle in Time — Book 2

Alice VL

PART FIVE

Holly lifted her head slightly when she heard a faint knock on her window. She looked over to her side window, and saw a bewildered Sarah calling for her. Holly rolled down her window, before she burst into tears.

"Holly, what's happened?" Sarah opened her car door, and at once, helped Holly out.

"She didn't make it. I took her to the hospital last night. They diagnosed her with congestive heart failure. They admitted her, but still, it wasn't enough?"

Sarah placed her arms around Holly, and left her to cry on her shoulders. She gently stroked Holly's back and was immensely saddened by her enormous grief. "Let's go inside ..."

Holly nodded her head, and followed Sarah through the wooden doors of Fine Books. When they walked in, Cindy hurriedly made her way to where they were standing. "Is everything alright, Sè?" Cindy was certain that the girl with Sarah, was Holly.

"Will you please stand in for me, mom?"

"Of course, my girl, take all the time you need …"

Sarah took Holly's hand, and led her into the reading lounge. She helped Holly onto a couch before she took a seat beside her. "I am so sorry, Holly. I am so sorry for your loss."

Holly swabbed at the tears that were relentlessly gushing from her eyes, and as she gasped for air in between her violent sobs. "I don't understand, Sarah?"

Sarah took in a deep breath, before she took Holly's hands, "I don't know how it works, Holly? I do know that it has something to do with a fault in the stars. Something about when the universe comes together and they all agree. Perhaps, you weren't meant to save your mother?"

"Then why send me back, Sarah. Why send me back to a day before my mother dies?"

"I don't know? Maybe it was so that you could finally understand that nothing you could have done would have saved her? Maybe you've been living with the guilt of your mother's death, and maybe, it's the universe's way of showing you that there was no fault in your mother's stars? Maybe Holly, it was so that you could forgive yourself for your mother's death? You did get one more last chance with her, Holly, you did all you could to save her. You saw the signs this time, and even though it didn't save her life, you did all you could. And Holly, you said goodbye ... even if you didn't actually say it."

"It's not enough, Sarah. I thought, I thought she'd be okay?" Holly's voice was breaking as the tears continued to stream down her cheeks.

Sarah hugged her tightly, and did her best to wipe the tears from her eyes.

"What do I do now, Sarah?"

"Now Holly, you do what you did once before. You carry on. You change your course, and you alter your own fate. You came back for a reason, and I can only assume that if it wasn't for your mother, it was for you and your child. You must focus on that now."

"I don't know how, Sarah?"

"I didn't either, Holly. I didn't know what to do, but I did learn to trust and have a little faith in the universe to step in and help me. You must too …"

"Adam is going to murder me, Sarah, and he's been a lifelong friend of Mark. I can't tell him any of this?"

"I know, but you must find a way to alter your course. You must avoid Adam at all cost."

"I can't. I've never like him, but he's always found a way into our lives. Mark loves him like a brother …"

"You must find a way, Holly. Your child's life depends on it. Your life depends on it."

"All I can do is to walk away from Mark. Break up with him, and move on with my life without him. Perhaps, he isn't my destiny. Perhaps, that was the fault in my stars before?"

Sarah hugged Holly one more time, "Oh Holly …"

"I have to call Mark and tell him about my mom. I should leave …"

"Is there anything I can do for you, Holly?"

"No, not really. I need to call the funeral home. I just can't believe that my mother is not my one more last chance. I thought she would be okay …"

"I know. I don't know what I'd do if something were to happen to my mom. I am here if you need me, Holly. I am always here."

Holly got up and when Sarah stood in front of her, Holly held her tightly against her. "Thank you, Sarah ..."

"You're welcome, Holly. I am so sorry."

"Thank you." Holly smiled sadly before she turned to leave.

Sarah followed closely behind her, and when she walked out through the doors of Fine Books, she hurriedly made her way back to Cindy.

"Was that Holly?"

"Yes, her mother passed away early this morning. She tried everything she could to save her mother. She thought that that was her one more last chance."

"Oh baby, is she going to be okay?"

"I think so, mom. I just don't think she came back to save her mother. I don't think her mother was her do-over. I think she might no longer feel guilt for her mother's death as she did in her old future, but I don't think she came back for her. I think she came back to save herself, mom, herself and her baby."

"Yes, I think so too, my girl. I hope she does ..."

"Me too. It's in a year or two from now, not quite sure, but at least she has time, and we can help her, right mom? If she needs us?"

Cindy placed her hand on Sarah's hair, and gently stroked it. "Of course, we can baby. Do you know what you can do for her now? You can write Holly's story for her."

"You think so? Oh, that's a wonderful idea. I am going to get started on that right now. Thanks mommy, I love you ..." Sarah planted a firm kiss on Cindy's forehead before she hurriedly made her way upstairs and into her study.

"I love you too!" Cindy shouted out behind her, before she disappeared up the stairs.

Alice VL

When Holly reached her mother's house, she sat down at the kitchen table and quickly dialed Mark's number.

"Hello beautiful?" When Holly heard his voice, she burst out crying. A curbing lump in her throat had abruptly silenced her, and all Mark could hear was uncontrollable sobbing.

"Holly?" He felt fear invade his entire being and his heart began to shudder profusely.

"She's gone …" It was all that Holly could say before she placed her phone on the table in front of her, and buried her head in her arms.

Holly's heart had shattered into a million pieces when she glanced around the kitchen and realized that she would never again hear the beautiful humming of her mother's voice.

There will never be another fresh bread baking in the oven, and never again will the teapot be ready for a cup of tea with her mother. Even though she had lived through the torment and pain of Danielle's death once before, there was nothing that could have prepared her for it a second time.

She was so sure that Danielle would recover. She was convinced that she would survive. There was nothing to indicate to Holly that all her efforts were in vain. She had returned one day before her mother's death, and still, there was nothing she could do to save her.

Mark became panicky at once, and without excusing himself from class, he rushed outside and ran down the path that led out to the parking lot. When he reached his car, he heard Adam's voice behind him, "Mark! Stop! What's going on?"

"I don't know. It's Holly! I must go to her!" He was frantic to unlock his car door and get out to Holly as soon as he could.

"I'll drive you, buddy?"

"No, I want to go alone. I'll call you later, okay?"

"Yeah, okay …"

When Mark finally unlocked his car door, he slid into the driver's seat, and started the car all in one motion. He sped out of the parking lot, desperate to reach Holly.

Mark pulled up into the driveway and ran over to her front door. Without knocking, he frantically opened the door, "Holly? Holly!" He called out to her as he made his way into their home.

"In the kitchen …"

He heard a husky, trembling voice echo down the hall before he realized it was coming from the kitchen. When Holly saw him in the doorway, she got up from her seat, and fell hopelessly into his arms. As though a fresh batch of tears had been waiting for Mark to arrive, they gushed from her eyes while clinging desperately onto him.

"I don't understand? I thought it was a routine check-up?" Mark whispered as though he had found himself in a dense, foggy mist. Holly sobbed and quivered violently, unable to speak as he held tightly onto her.

When her tears began to soak his sweater, Holly backed away slightly, and desperately tried to wipe the wave of tears that had drowned out her face. She hunched slightly as she made her way back to an empty chair at the kitchen table.

Mark pulled out a chair right beside her and took her hands into his. He stared at her, waiting for her to compose herself.

"It was. It was just a check-up, but then, they discovered that she was in the late stages of congestive heart failure."

Mark bowed his head and squeezed her hands tighter.

"They admitted her and said that, that she'd be okay. That the treatment should slow it down, and then, then I came home ..." Holly's tears continued to gush from her eyes, as she swallowed back on that ever restricting, and confining lump in her throat.

"They, called me and said that she didn't make it. She's gone, Mark. My mommy is gone! And I, I was here. She died all alone!" Holly's tears were once more, drowning out her face, and when she became silent, Mark knew that her entire world was falling apart around her.

"I am so sorry, baby, so sorry." He knelt in front of her and pulled her closer to him. He left her to cry, his own heart shattering by the pain and torment he was witnessing in her.

"I mean, Holly, how could they not have picked this up sooner?"

Holly grabbed a serviette from the table, and irately wiped at the tears that were incessantly flowing from her eyes. "She's, I mean, she never said anything. She never complained. She was getting out of breath, and she seemed more tired than normal. Mom picked up a bit of weight in the last few months, but, I just thought that she was getting older, you know?"

Mark nodded sadly, "Yeah."

"She was due for her yearly check-up next month, but she wouldn't have lived until then …"

Mark got up and pulled her up with him. He placed his arms around her waist and held her protectively against him. "I'm sorry, Holly …"

"I know, Mark. I know you were as fond of her as she was of you." She held him tightly, and again, she could not deny the shelter his arms had offered her. Holly felt safe in his arms. She felt loved by him, and when she rested her head on his chest, she was comforted by the beating of his heart.

"Do you want to get some rest?"

Holly drew slightly back when she was once again reminded of the events that would take place in a few short years from that very moment.

"Yes. I want to be alone. I have calls to make. I need to contact the funeral home and arrange for my mother's body to be picked up. There's just too much to do …"

"I can stay, and we can make those calls together?"

Holly turned around and hurriedly placed her coffee mug in the basin. "No, I just want to be alone for a bit …"

Mark walked over to her, her back turned to him, and placed his arms around her shoulders. "Call me if you need me, alright? For anything, call me."

She turned around and smiled despondently at him, "Thank you …" She whispered hoarsely as she swallowed back on a brand-new batch of tears that had announced their arrival.

Holly ran up the stairs and into her mother's bedroom. She listened closely as Mark started his car, and pulled out of the driveway. When she could no longer hear the roaring of his pick-up, she sat on the edge of her mother's bed. Holly glanced around her, and became tearful when she noticed, almost for the first time, how neat and organized her mother was.

On her dresser, she proudly displayed the perfume bottles she had collected, and filled over the years. Behind them was a photograph of her father, Arthur, and next to that photograph, was another of the three of them when Holly was only a baby. Her hairbrush laid neatly on the dresser, as though Danielle had just brushed her hair. Her hair clips were neatly placed in a glass jar, and her lipstick was deftly organized in a handmade shelf Arthur had once made for her.

Holly glanced over to her closet, and slowly made her way to the shut doors. She opened them one by one, and stood back to pore over the clothes her mother had once worn. She moved closer and gently touched the rows and rows of dresses that were hanging gracefully side by side.

She leaned in to one of her blouses and closed her eyes. Holly took in a deep breath and beamed when the aroma of her mother's familiar scent entirely engulfed her, and travelled throughout her whole body.

Holly closed the closet doors, and turned back to the oversized bed right in the center of Danielle's bedroom. It was unmade, bearing evidence that Holly had slept there only hours before. She walked over to the bed, and swiftly made Danielle's bed.

"Mom would be so mad …" She whispered to herself knowing that Danielle would be horrified if she had to stumble upon an unmade bed. Holly's eyes caught a glimpse of her nightstand. She smiled sadly at the collection of books that were neatly stacked behind a lamp.

"A Moment in Time by Sarah Swanson." Holly whispered when she noticed the familiar title. Sarah Swanson had married Daniel Kingsley on the day she had read that book for the very first time. Danielle had continuously nagged Holly to read Sarah's story and all she had been through.

Holly grew increasingly agitated with Danielle, and finally relented. When she had turned the last page of the book, Danielle was eager for Holly's opinion.

"I think this is a whole lot of mumbo jumbo … people don't go back in time! It's impossible!"

"Nonsense Holly! Anything is possible if you believe."

"Yeah, right."

While Holly stood staring at Sarah's book, she heard an unexpected thud on her front door. Holly frowned before she turned away, and hurriedly made her way downstairs.

She reached the front door just as there was a second knock, and when she opened the door, she was at once caught off-guard when she saw Adam Weston standing there. Even before he had attacked her, she was anxious and entirely unsettled around him.

There was something about him that sent convulsions running up and down her spine. Knowing at that moment what she knew, she became profoundly fearful and apprehensive when he appeared at her front door.

"Adam? What are you doing here?" She whispered croakily, unsure of what to do or what to say to him.

"I heard about your mother. I thought I'd stop by and offer my condolences."

Holly forced a smile, but could in no way at all, shake a feeling of dread that had begun to overwhelm her. "Thank you."

She smiled again and was about to close the door, when he pressed his hand against it.

"Can I come in?"

"I, I have so many arrangements to make, it's just not a good time ..."

"It'll only be for a minute?"

Holly did not want to anger Adam. She had to force herself to remain friendly and composed around him, at least until Danielle's funeral was over.

Holly moved out the way for Adam to walk in. She nervously closed the door behind him, and stood in the doorway, ready to run out through her front door if the moment called for it.

The horror that had suddenly invaded her entire being, was nothing compared to the utter revulsion she felt for him at that very moment. "Does Mark know you're here?" Holly whispered, suddenly aware of an overshadowing shudder in her voice.

"I am sure he'll appreciate my support, don't you think?"

Holly knew that there was something not quite right with Adam. It was something she couldn't put a finger on, but as she stood staring at him, she was sure that she was looking into the eyes of the devil.

There was no doubt in her mind that it was pure evil standing right in front of her. Adam moved closer to her, and placed his arms around her. He pulled her tightly against him and pressed her head into his chest. "Again, so sorry for your loss …" Holly's heart began to race when he forced her against him. She was at once taken back to that exact moment once before. She had not yet known what she had learnt since. She thought that he was nothing more than young and extremely foolish, but this time, Holly knew exactly what was coming next.

Holly tried to free herself from his grip, before she looked up and into his eyes. It was a look she had recognized, one she had seen twice before. She saw it for the very first time at that very moment, in another time, and she saw it again the night he murdered her.

Adam grabbed her face, and pressed his lips against hers. Holly did not struggle as she did before. Her heart began to batter abundantly, as she prayed for the moment to be over soon.

When he finally released her, Holly stepped back and turned to the front door. She opened the door and smiled at Adam, "Thank you for stopping by, Adam. It was nice to see you again."

Adam was wholly unprepared for her reaction and frowned, absolutely stunned by Holly's unexpected response. "You do want me? I knew it!"

Adam walked up to her and placed his hand around her as he firmly clasped her bottom and squeezed it. "Adam, my mother just died. I am with Mark. I love Mark. I do, so I don't know why you think that, but I love you as a friend. What you did just now was stupid, but, we won't speak of it again."

She engaged in a courageous endeavor to remain composed and friendly. She was terrified of Adam, and she was deathly afraid that he might turn into an enraged psychopath.

"I really have to call the funeral home now. Thank you for stopping by. I so appreciate your friendship and support."

Again, Adam was stunned by her nonchalant attitude. He grimaced at her, and when he looked at her one last time, Holly could see the wrath that had begun to slowly build in his eyes. "I hope for your sake you're not patronizing me?"

Holly knew that she would stutter the moment she opened her mouth, so she remained silent and shook her head gently. When he walked out, she quickly closed the door behind him, and locked it at once.

Holly ran around to the kitchen door, and quickly closed the latch. She peered over at all the opening windows and was relieved that they were securely closed. When she stood against the wall, she slowly slid to her knees.

She had no idea how to prevent what would inevitably happen to her in the not too distant future. The only thing she was certain of, was that she would have to cut ties with Adam entirely, and the only way to do that, was to cut ties with Mark too.

The very thought of losing Mark brought Holly to tears. It felt as though a dagger had been piercing her heart over and over, and that the pain she was feeling was almost too much to stand. There were no winners.

There was no way at all that she could let Mark go, and carry on as though he never was. In her struggle to remain strong and to survive, her true torment began. She had never felt as isolated as she had at that very moment.

All she felt was sorrow as every single pleasurable emotion she had felt before was banished from her heart, her mind and her soul. Where there once was love and joy, was now filled with an aching hollowness she knew she could never quite get used to. She did not want to acquaint herself with the nothingness that had introduced itself to her, but there was nothing Holly could do than to walk away from Mark and eliminate Adam from her now and from her future.

THE BOOKSTORE SERIES
A Crinkle in Time – Book 2

Alice VL

PART SIX

In the days after the funeral, Holly bravely attempted to return to her normal routine. She returned to class when she realized in shock that she had less than four months left before she was to graduate.

It was her mother's one wish for Holly to graduate from college, and she was determined to do it, if only for her. Holly compared her heartbreak to a grief that would hit her in waves. It was grueling. There were times when she thought that she could barely get through the day, and there were days she conquered effortlessly.

Those were the days that saved her, the days she found renewed strength to carry with her through to another bad day that would wait for her just around the next corner. She had lost her appetite and she had barely slept at night.

Holly had locked up her mother's bedroom door, and spent most of her time in her own, entirely shut off from the world. She threw herself into her studies, and took time to mourn and grieve her mother.

Holly would lay awake at night staring at the ceiling, as she replayed Danielle's last night repeatedly. It was different to before. Her mother had not died in her bed, but in a hospital where she was sure they would save her.

She was secretly thankful that she had done all she could to save her, yet, she still could not help but wonder why she was forced to relive her mother's painful death one more time, as though the first time was not enough.

She kept reflecting on what Sarah had told her, and although she was reluctant to admit it, Holly knew that she had never before forgiven herself for her mother's untimely death the first time.

Perhaps it was time to forgive herself. Perhaps, it was time that she realized that not she, nor all the doctors and money in the world, could have saved her mother. Perhaps, the only fault in the stars was Holly's guilt, and her subsequent inability to forgive herself.

She would ponder endlessly on Danielle's funeral. It was beautiful and just as she was sure, her mother would have wanted.

Even though the weather was perfect on that sunny morning, everything around her seemed as grey, cold and damp as a reflection of her emotions.

She was angry that the birds continued to sing, and that the flowers were beginning to bloom. She struggled to suppress her grief as her tears flowed steadily from her eyes. She felt bruised inside, a numbness and emptiness she never wanted to feel again.

She followed her mother's beautiful white coffin until it was lowered into the ground. She begged the undertaker to be careful and gentle with her, for the body he was carrying was her mother, and she hated to see her placed into the ground.

The words from the minister sounded to her as though he was speaking in a language she did not understand. The onslaught of tears around her, from close friends and loved ones of Danielle, were meant to be a confirmation and tribute of her life, but all it did was remind her that she would never see her beloved mother again.

People were dressed in black. Some brought flowers, others brought hugs. When the grave diggers began closing her grave, Holly was sure that a fragment of her heart was buried with her.

She was comforted by the fact that Sarah and Daniel Kingsley had attended Danielle's funeral. She found solace in the knowing that Sarah could relate to what she was going through, even though the rest of the world would not quite understand.

"I am so sorry, Holly ..." Sarah embraced Holly and held her snugly against her as she tried her utmost to comfort her.

"Thank you for coming, Sarah. I feel so alone, and people here don't understand. They don't know ..."

"I know, Holly. But, I am here for you, and so is Daniel and my mother. Whatever you need, okay?"

She let go of Holly, before Daniel placed his arms around her. "We are here for you. We've been down this road before. Whatever you need, Holly, we are just a phone call or a bookstore away." Daniel smiled sadly before he stepped back, and took Sarah's hand.

"Remember what I said, Holly. You were given a chance to let go of the guilt surrounding your mother's death. It's time to forgive yourself. Take time to mourn her. Take all the time you need, and then, then you must focus on what is still to come.

Okay?" Holly nodded sadly as a lost tear rolled down her cheek.

Holly was indebted to Sarah and Daniel for their empathy, compassion and kindness. She was deeply grateful that Sarah had come into her life, and without question or doubt, she took her hand, and hadn't yet let go. She knew that she would have to deny her feelings for Mark, but all she could focus on at that very moment, was to come to terms with her mother's passing, and to get through her final few months at college.

Mark came by often to check on her, but she declined all invitations to dinner or even a day out with him. On more occasions than she cared to admit, Adam accompanied Mark to her house, but Holly would cut their visits abruptly short.

She avoided eye contact with Adam as much as possible, and would respond to him by shrugging him off. She refused to let him catch a glimpse of the uneasiness in her that he alone was responsible for.

Mark could not shake the feeling that Holly was wholly uncomfortable around Adam, and he would question her when she treated him, what he deemed to be as unfair, "I don't get why you don't like Adam? Sure, he's got a big mouth, but he's a really good guy, Holly?"

"I don't like him, Mark. I just don't. There's something wrong with him!"

They would end up having heated arguments over Adam, and it would end when Mark would leave, slamming her front door behind him.

Mark excused her behavior as a side effect of grieving Danielle. He was convinced that her longing for her mother was responsible for her resentment towards Adam. Mark made an effort to be more understanding and patient with her, as she navigated through the grief, trying as hard as he could to support her.

It bothered him tremendously that she no longer left the house, other than to attend her classes at college. On occasion, she would tell him that she was at Fine Books, where she would supposedly research an upcoming project or test, but other than that, she refused to go anywhere with him, especially when Adam was around.

Holly felt safe, shielded and relaxed at Fine Books, and in the presence of Sarah and Cindy. She would pop in as often as she could, and simply sit and talk with Sarah from early morning until late afternoon.

On one particular visit, Sarah told Holly about the book she had started writing, A Crinkle in Time. "So, Holly, I have been meaning to discuss something with you?"

"Okay?" Holly frowned when she noticed the uncertainty in Sarah's eyes.

"You know that I wrote A Moment in Time based on my own experience with Passage of Time and Adelaine Alandrali? I thought that perhaps you and I could work on your story too?"

Holly's eyes grew wider as she considered it for a moment. "Yeah, we could. I just don't know how it ends?"

"I know. I didn't either. We can work on it until the time comes? What do you say? It would be something you can one day look back on?"

"Okay. I mean, if I survive? But, I would love it if you write it?"

"We're going to make sure you survive, Holly. You didn't come back here just to die all over again. I would love to write it for you. I've taken the liberty of naming it, Adelaine Alandrali's, A Crinkle in Time?"

"I love that!"

Alice VL

THE BOOKSTORE SERIES
A Crinkle in Time – Book 2

"Oh good. So, we'll get together whenever you can and work on it together?"

"Thank you for this, Sarah, thank you for always being here for me." Holly smiled sadly, and could once again sense a feeling of tranquility and peace around Sarah.

Alice VL

THE BOOKSTORE SERIES
A Crinkle in Time – Book 2

The day after Holly, Adam and Mark graduated from college, Mark had applied to become a fire fighter in Hazel Creek. Much to her displeasure, and even though she had expected it and knew it, Adam applied to the academy too.

When they both were accepted, Mark could hardly contain his excitement, "I can't wait to start, Holly. And when I get back, we should get an apartment together, are you game?"

Holly was once again ill-equipped for the way in which fate was coming back to haunt her. "How long will you be in training for?"

"We leave on Sunday evening for Queenstown. It's six weeks of vigorous training, and if we pass our physical training, we'll spend another two weeks with practical training. So, in total, it looks like eight weeks."

Holly took in a breath of fresh air before she let out a disheartening sigh. She was at once relieved that Mark and Adam would both be gone for two months. It would give her an opportunity to spend more time with Sarah, as she decides how to best move forward with her life, and how to best use the time she was given for her one more last chance.

But, she could no longer pretend that Mark was an enormous fraction of her future. It was the one fragment of her

Alice VL

life that she was forced to remove and put behind her. A future without Mark was all that made sense to her, and the events that would someday shatter both their lives.

She loved Mark dearly, and since Danielle's passing, he had stood unwaveringly by her side, but Holly knew the gruesomeness of the scene that would someday await him, would be too much for Mark to bear.

There was no point in dragging it out, and she hoped that his time away from Hazel Creek and from her, would be the time he would need to come to terms with their breakup.

"I'm happy for you, Mark. I truly am. It's been a dream of yours for so long, but ..."

Mark frowned when he detected the gentle quiver in her voice. "But?"

"I just, I think that we should just take a break. I am exhausted, and my mother's death has just made me reevaluate certain aspects of my life, you know?"

"What do you mean? A break? From each other?"

Holly lowered her head and clasped her hands together. "I just think that with you being there, and me being here, we should take the time away to be without one another?"

"Why?"

"I just want to be alone for a while. With my mother gone, I am not even sure I want to stay here in Hazel Creek anymore. I don't know what I want to do with my life, and I don't want you to have to cope with that now. I just think that maybe we've just, outgrown one another?"

"What exactly are you saying, Holly? I love you. I don't want to be away from you. I haven't outgrown you. Have you outgrown me?"

She looked into his eyes, and when she noticed the utter desolation staring back to her, she was sure that her heart was about to shatter into a thousand scrappy pieces.

She loved Mark. She had loved Mark from the moment she had met him. He was the man she would dream of at night and the first thing she would think of when she awoke in the mornings. His voice was what made her heart flutter. The way he looked at her, would make her stomach turn. When he touched her, she was sure that butterflies from all over the world had settled into her stomach.

She wondered for a moment, if she would be able to pull it off, and tell Mark that she was no longer sure if she loved him. "I'm, I'm just not sure how I feel anymore, Mark? I don't know if our direction is the direction I want to take?"

Mark turned away from her before he ran his fingers through his hair. Holly was horrified by the devastation that had made its way into his eyes.

When he turned back to her, he placed his hands on her shoulders, "Holly. Don't do this. You are still so broken up about your mother. Just give yourself time. Please, don't do this, not now. I know things are hard for you at the moment, and I know it has only been you and your mother for so long, but Holly, you cannot make decisions like this when you are hurting."

She traced his lips with the tips of her fingers. She had an overwhelming urge to kiss them, and all she wanted was to ask him to hold her in his arms. Holly placed her hand on his cheek and decided that her performance would be the best performance she would ever be bound to give.

"Mark. You are such a good man. You are kind. You are so attractive. I like you, so much, but I don't, I don't think it's enough? I don't think it's really earth-shattering, butterflies kind of love. And I am sorry. I feel like such a bad person for saying that. You've been here for me every step of the way. You've stood by me, comforted me and you've been such an amazing friend, but we sort of settled into that, you know? A friendship, and one I value with all my heart …"

Mark interrupted her before she could carry on, "You don't love me? When did this happen?"

"I don't know? I think when my mom died, it just forced me to take stock of my feelings, you know?"

"Wow! I did not see this coming. Now? A few days before I leave, you tell me this?" Mark placed both his hands on his head before he turned away from her one more time.

"I am sorry, Mark. I don't want to hurt you …"

When he turned back to her, Holly was horrified to notice the tears that were beginning to glisten in his eyes. She could no longer stand to look at him. Her heart broke out into an enormous gallop, and she was afraid that if he stood there for only a moment longer, she would relent and admit that she was lying to save her own life.

"I have nothing more to say about this, Mark. I would

appreciate it if you rather just leave. In time, you'll see that this was the right thing to do, and what is best for both of us. Before we get married. Before we have children someday. This is the only way for us, before we make mistakes we can't recover from."

He frowned again when he detected the utter frostiness in her voice. Without responding to her, and as though overcome with shock, he lifted his keys from the kitchen table, and left.

When he reached his pick-up, he climbed into the driver's seat and sat staring at her house for much longer than he should have. He could never in his wildest dreams have imagined that Holly's heart would turn so coldly against him. It was something he never thought he would hear her say, and yet, when he stood in front of her only moments before, she couldn't have been any clearer.

As his tears began to trickle from his eyes, he was sure that his heart had splintered into a hundred little shards. There was no indication in the days leading up to that moment to tell him that Holly Mackenzie no longer loved him.

She had grown distant and removed from him, but he thought it was her sorrow and grief, and her frantic need to cope with her mother's death.

When he thought about their last few days together, he reluctantly admitted to himself that the signs were there, he just never saw them. He never wanted to see them. She no longer spent a night with him, and she no longer accepted invitations from him. They hadn't watched a movie together in weeks, and they had not shared one meal together since Danielle passed away.

Her words hit him as hard as nails that were being hammered into his heart. It hardly felt real to him, almost as though he was stuck in a nightmare he couldn't wake up from. Mark was hurt, but more than anything else, he was entirely beleaguered by her betrayal.

She no longer joined him for football games, and when he would check in on her at home, she was uncomfortable around him. She would perhaps share one cup of coffee with him, before she made an excuse for him to leave.

Mark was devastated that he failed to see the signs, and he was crushed when he heard her tell him that she no longer loved him. Before he pulled out of her driveway, he was sure that perhaps Holly, simply needed time to figure out her feelings and find her place in a world without her mother.

He thought that perhaps, distance was what she needed and that her emotions were overshadowing her true feelings for him.

Alice VL

PART SEVEN

Holly cried herself to sleep the night Mark walked out of her front door for the last time. She tossed, and she turned when she thought of Mark's training in the city. She prayed for his safety, and she prayed that her heart would no longer suffer the agonizing pain of losing him.

When he finally left for the city a few days later, she was forced to control every part of her that nudged her to see him off at the fire station. She took her phone on more occasions than one, desperate to send him a text message, but each time she began, she erased her words, and tossed her mobile phone in anger.

There was no other way. There was nothing else she could do to change the sequence of events that would take place in a few short years. She could hardly tell Mark the truth, and she could not accuse Adam of a crime that he had not yet committed, a crime that had not yet taken place. Holly was shattered by having to have made that decision, and she prayed that somehow, her heart would forgive her, and find someone else to love someday.

What she couldn't tell Mark was that there was an honesty behind all her lies and betrayal. There was a concealed pain festering inside of her for what the future would unavoidably hold for them, had she not had the courage to walk away from him.

At the very moment he walked out of her door, her world had collapsed one more time. The light that had shone so brightly into her heart, had become a shadow filled with torture and agony.

While Mark, Adam and a dozen other trainees gathered at the fire station in Hazel Creek, waiting for a bus to pick them up, Holly drove into town, and pulled up at Fine Books.

She was desperate to speak to Sarah. She was frantic to hear Sarah tell her that she did the right thing. Her heart needed validation and her soul needed to understand.

When she walked in, she did not hear the chiming of the bell. The world had become noisy around her, and the demons of what lay ahead had begun to invade her.

Alice VL

When she saw Sarah and Cindy behind the counter, Holly burst into tears, overcome with utter devastation. She at once covered her face with her hands, and cried from the very core of her soul.

Cindy hurriedly made her way over to Holly, and placed her arms around her, "Oh baby …" She pulled her closer and held her tightly against her. "I know. I know it hurts …"

When Sarah joined them, Cindy let go of Holly and gently wiped the tears from her eyes, "You must be strong, Holly. This is your one more last chance. This is it. This is all you'll ever have to get it right."

Holly nodded, while she frenetically swabbed at the tears on her cheeks.

"Come on, let's go to the lounge. Mom, will you order hot chocolate drinks for us please?" Sarah turned back to her mother as they made their way into the lounge.

"Sure baby …" Cindy smiled before she walked back around the counter.

Sarah and Holly took their places on the couch in the reading lounge where Sarah handed her a box of tissues and left her to cry for as long as she needed to.

Cindy had brought in two mugs of steaming hot chocolate and quietly placed them on the coffee table in front of the couch. When her tears began to subside, Sarah handed her a mug of hot chocolate as she sipped on her own.

"Do you want to talk about it, Holly?" Sarah whispered while sipping slowly on her drink.

"He leaves for the city today ..."

"Mark?"

"Yeah ..."

"He'll be back soon, Holly, you'll see ..."

"It's not that Sarah, it's, I told him I don't love him and never want to see him again ..."

Sarah placed her mug on the coffee table, before she moved closer to Holly and gently stroked her hair. "Isn't there another way, Holly?"

"I don't see another way, Sarah. As long as Adam is around, my fate has been decided. Mark and I have been fighting non-stop over Adam. He will never believe me if I tell him the truth. I don't want to do that to Mark. I don't want Mark to find me like that. Murdered in our own home and by his best friend. I don't want the autopsy to reveal that we were going to have a baby, I can't do that to him. And he does find me, Sarah."

Sarah took her hand and held it tightly in her own hand.

"I don't want to be raped, beaten and stabbed, Sarah. I can still smell the tobacco and whiskey on his breath. Some nights, I wake up and smell the stale and staunch whiff of blood all around me. My own blood. I can feel the dampness on me, and I can't imagine Mark finding me like that. I hate that man so much. I curse the day Adam was born!"

"I know, Holly, and I am so sorry it happened to you. Maybe your heart will understand, just give it some time. You've just lost your mother, you've just graduated from college and now Mark, it's a lot to handle and try and cope with. Give yourself some time. Maybe a better solution will present itself to you in future, you never know? You must have faith, Holly." She paused to take in a deep breath, "I thought I failed when I couldn't change Daniel's destiny. I thought that it was all for nothing, you know? It turned out, I just needed to have faith in him. I needed to believe that he would see the signs, and he did, Holly. Even though it was at the very last minute, he saw the signs. He never believed me, and his sister, Margie, she never believed me, but in the end and with hardly any time to spare, they all saw it. Believe that Mark will see them too ..."

Holly looked up and gazed into Sarah's eyes, "How can he know anything of signs, and how can I ask him to believe me when I haven't even told him? You know how crazy this sounds, Sarah? I mean, the first time I read your book, I thought you were a nut job. But you know what is so ironic, Sarah? My mother believed in you. She begged me to read your book, you know?"

"Have you tried telling Mark about all this? That you came back?"

Holly shook her head, "No, he will never believe me. Mark has only one way of thinking, and that doesn't include anything supernatural like ghosts, or things like that. He will never believe that I came back. He doesn't even watch movies that have anything supernatural in them."

"Nobody believed me either, Holly. Everyone thought that I was a crazy person. Daniel's patience was beginning to wear thin, but when it came time for him to see the signs, he did. He saw them, and he's never doubted me since. I just couldn't give up. I took every opportunity I had to try and make him understand the things I knew."

Holly frowned slightly, "And your mama, Sarah?"

"My mama was skeptical at first, and I didn't even realize I told her the names of my niece and nephew, but when I did, she asked my sister who gave her the exact same names. So, you have to keep trying, Holly, even when no-one believes you. You must."

Holly wiped her nose with a fresh tissue before she turned back to Sarah, "I don't have the guts to, Sarah. I am so afraid to. It feels like I must defend myself against the truth, like I'm trapped and imprisoned by the borders of honesty. I'm not strong like you, Sarah, I can't stick to the something that sounds so ridiculous!"

"Oh Holly, you are so much stronger than you think. You'll realize that when being strong is the only option you have."

Holly rested her head against Sarah's shoulder, before she closed her eyes. She thought of Mark, and she thought of how empty her life was all of a sudden. She never intended to break his heart, and she never thought her heart could hurt as it did at that very moment.

She loved Mark. She adored the man who made her feel like a princess, but she could not discard the memory of the scene he came home to in a few years from that day.

She could never put him through that again, and she never wanted to relive the brutality that Adam had inflicted upon her and her unborn child.

Alice VL

PART EIGHT

In the weeks that followed Mark's departure to the city, Holly busied herself by turning a second living room into her design studio. She had signed two clients, and decided to distract herself from Mark, and plunge herself head, heart and soul first into her work.

She had converted the living room into a modern, functioning and beautiful studio where she took out an outside wall and replaced it with glass. Each time she lifted her eyes, she had a perfect view of her garden. Each time she gazed out at the beautiful scenery that awaited her, she couldn't quite grasp how her life had changed in just a few short weeks.

She had lost her mother, and she had said goodbye to Mark. She would sit at her desk, and gaze out over the apple tree that was nothing more than a mess of unruly twigs only a few weeks ago. They were beginning to bloom, and Holly would smile each time she noticed buds appear on all the branches. It was early summer, and the naked trees were now resurrected as though new life had been breathed into them.

The rain came down hard the past few days, but when it finally stopped, buds began appearing all over the garden, and the grass turned green almost overnight.

Holly had ripped out the scuffed and worn carpet, and replaced it with wooden flooring, with a few scattered rugs over them. She had a carpenter come in and add shelves to the walls where she proudly displayed all her projects. She would often stand in the doorway, and admire the beautiful studio she was able to spend most of her days in.

Holly had slowly begun packaging and boxing away her mother's clothes, shoes and most of her most intimate belongings. She had replaced her curtains and bedding, and packed away her perfume bottles.

The photo albums Danielle had kept in her closet, were now being kept on shelves in her studio where Holly could glance over the hundreds of photographs whenever her longing for her mother became too much to bear.

Holly moved into her mother's bedroom, and turned hers into a spare bedroom which she hoped to convert into a nursery someday.

Her dreams had not ended, even though her dream with Mark did. She often stared at the stars late at night, and wondered if she would ever meet someone to love again.

She wanted someone whose eyes she could get lost in until the beating of his heart transformed itself into her surroundings. She wanted to fall in love with his hair, his eyes and his body. She wanted to see his faults as his perfections, his words as her thoughts and lock her heart into his forever. As she sat gazing out at the stars, Holly knew that her dreams kept shoving Mark's eyes into her mind. She had a nagging and unsettling feeling that Mark would be the only man she would ever love.

But, Holly knew that she had to try. She never planned on growing old alone. She wanted the family she had dreamed of for most of her life. She wanted someone to love her, even though she would never stop loving Mark. She wanted it all, and she was sure that if enough time had passed, she would learn to love another. She would learn to cherish him and the life she hoped they would someday share. She would learn to devote herself to him, just as she had once dedicated herself to Mark.

Alice VL

THE BOOKSTORE SERIES
A Crinkle in Time – Book 2

Mark arrived in Queenstown on a cold, windy night almost a thousand miles away from Hazel Creek. They had barely stepped of the bus when torrential rain attacked the streets of Queenstown.

The bright city lights seemed blurred as lightning spat all around them. When Mark looked up into the night sky at the thunder rolling across the heavens, he was sure that it could crack the entire world in half.

He hated the city, and he hated being so far from Hazel Creek. He was relieved that Adam was with him, and he prayed for distraction from Holly, even though he could barely get her off his mind.

Each time he would think of her, it would feel to him as though a sharp knife had been plunged into his heart. He felt betrayed and discarded by her. Still, no matter how desperate he was to banish her from his mind, all he could think of was Holly.

After one of their training sessions a few days later, Mark and Adam snuck out of their dorm for a quick smoke break in the courtyard close to their dorms.

"You heard from Holly yet?" Adam could hardly contain his curiosity.

"Nope. I told you, she wants nothing more to do with me?"

"Oh dude! I thought you were kidding?"

"No. No jokes. She broke up with me just before we left."

"Oh man. What a bitch. This sucks!"

"Don't call her that Adam …"

Mark was at once irritated by Adam's insult.

"She is a fucking bitch, Mark. I never liked her you know? There was always something slutty about her, and I never, ever thought she was good enough for you."

Mark tossed his cigarette before he grabbed Adam by his collar, "Don't you ever call her that again! And just so you know, she can't stand you either!" Mark glared at him before he let go of Adam. He took two steps back before he turned to go back indoors.

"Sorry buddy! I didn't mean it like that!" Adam shouted out before Mark disappeared through the door.

When Mark reached his bed, he took out his mobile phone and instinctively, he sent her a text message, "Just checking in to see if you're okay?" When he hit the send button, he immediately regretted his decision.

In Hazel Creek, Holly had just turned in for the night when she noticed the flickering of the message light on her phone. She quickly unlocked the screen, and when she saw Mark's name, her heart almost missed a beat.

She sat straight up staring at his message for what felt like forever. She missed him. She longed for him, and she worried about him. She hated the fact that he was in Queenstown, and when she read his message one more time, Holly realized that she was her own worst enemy.

She was torn between her feelings for Mark and her destiny. She hated that she had to choose, and she despised the fact that it was all Adam's fault. Her mind drifted back to the night that Adam had assaulted her. She could not banish the cold look that mirrored his face directly onto hers.

There was no sense of humanity as he stabbed her over and over again. His heart had turned to stone, and the evil glint in his eyes was something Holly could never forget. Not only did he smell like whiskey and tobacco, he smelled of danger and death.

The worst thing for Holly to live with is the fact that nobody would ever suspect Adam of her murder. He appeared normal to the world. There was no sign, no indication and no warning at all of the monster that was lurking inside of him.

As Holly looked back on the years she had known Adam, she realized how well he had hidden his penchant for causing pain. But, the signs were always there. His anger was out of control so often, that he would take out his rage on an animal.

Often, Mark would have to step in as he tried to calm Adam down after a fit of sudden fury. He would hurl his mobile phone against a wall each time he was rejected, and leave the shattered pieces on the ground for someone else to pick up.

Holly was afraid of Adam, but what she was even more frightened of was the fact that Adam would undoubtedly kill someday. She was terrified for the woman that would find herself on Adam's path, and realize too late that he would become her very own boogeyman. There was nothing Holly could do to warn the world of the evil that would expose itself to the someone someday.

Her hatred for him had grown, and her disgust for him had multiplied in the weeks leading up to her break up with Mark.

At times, she was desperate to tell Mark the truth, and then there were times that she fantasized about stabbing him in his heart with a butcher's knife.

Each time the thought would cross Holly's mind, she felt an ice-cold shiver run down her spine, and immediately banished those evil and wicked thoughts from her mind.

Mark would persistently send short text messages to her. He would tell her about the grueling training on scourging hot days, and then again, on icy cold days. He made a comment about how unpredictable the weather was, and how they went through four entire seasons in one single day.

He would tell her how he hated the city, and how he could never leave Hazel Creek behind. He told her that he missed her, and that he would love her for the remainder of her life, even though she no longer loved him.

He begged her to search her heart and a place deep inside of her where love lived, perhaps she would find him there again. He pleaded with her to reconsider her decision, and then he asked her if she perhaps, missed him too.

Holly would re-read each message he sent to her over and over again. It was all she had to cling to, and all she had to mend her shattered heart and crushed spirit.

She so desperately wanted to run up to him and fling her arms around him when he was to return, and then, she wanted to tell him how sorely she missed him.

She wanted to reply to his texts, and tell him how dearly she loved him, but each time she came close to surrendering to her heart, she was reminded of another time, in a future, where Mark would find her lifeless body. She never responded to his messages, and she believed into the very center part of her core that her future could not include Mark.

As long as Adam was alive, Mark could be no part of her life. There was a sadness inside of Holly she knew she would never quite recover from.

The hardest part of walking away from him, was the reality that there was no other option available to her. For decades to come, Holly would be trapped in a world of what-ifs with Mark. For centuries after she leaves her world someday, her tears for Mark would continue to flow into the rivers and oceans of the earth.

The torment of his messages overwhelmed her with an explicable kind of suffering. She was never ready to say goodbye to him, but Holly would never be ready to die at the hands of a cold-blooded, heartless beast.

By the time February came around, Holly had confidently established herself as a graphics designer by offering her services to prospective clients as trial services initially, and without pay.

A few days before Christmas, she received a large order for Christmas cards from a local gift shop in Hazel Creek. She worked all day and all night to have them ready two days before Christmas, and when she delivered them on schedule, Cardalot assured her of many more, and bigger orders in future.

Holly slowly and cautiously began finding her feet and established a routine which made her feel safe as she returned to a new kind of normal. It would never be the normal she once knew, but it was a normal she had created and tailor-made for herself, a normal without her mother, and without Mark.

But, it was also a new, peaceful kind of normal without Adam. She thought of Mark often, but no longer received any text messages from him. She would go through photographs of him when she felt the longing almost too much to tolerate. Her aching for him came and went, but always returned during the quietest of moments at night.

Moments when the world around her became silent, and there was nothing more than the sounds of the night to keep her company. Her own passage of time had begun dulling the pain of his absence as her brain redirected itself to her work and reinvested her heart's energy into it.

When Holly glanced over at her diary in the early hours of February 12th, 2003, she realized that Mark would be back in Hazel Creek soon. She was not sure when they were scheduled to return, but when she roughly calculated his time away, she was sure that his expected arrival was within the next few days.

Her heart began to hammer fiercely at the mere thought of having him back in Hazel Creek, back on the streets they knew so well and the little town they both adored.

She was ghastly afraid of running into him, and she warned Sarah that her visits to Fine Books would be planned and coordinated to fit in with Mark's work schedule.

Holly closed her diary, and quickly poured herself her first cup of coffee for the day. She hurriedly made her way back into her studio, and sat behind her desk before she switched on her computer.

Each morning and without fail, Holly would first check her email messages, drink her coffee, and then complete an existing project, or begin a new one.

Alice VL

She was relieved to be able to keep busy so effortlessly, and she was grateful that her client base had grown so enormously, allowing her to fill her days with work. She gazed out to the back of her house, and stared out over the fields that were filled with daffodils and daisies during that time of the year.

She glanced over at the birds that were resting on a feeder, and she smiled at the beautiful sounds they would make. They were sounds that would remind her of the gentle humming of her mother that could be heard throughout their home.

She was still deep in thought when she heard a faint knock at her front door. Holly frowned in bewilderment. There were never any visitors to her house, and clients would be met at their premises. She quickly placed her mug on her desk, and swiftly made her way to her front door.

When she opened the door, she unexpectedly gasped for air when she saw him standing there, dressed in his fire fighter's uniform. She was completely unprepared to find Mark standing at her front door, and she had no inkling of how to react.

Her heart began to pound fiercely as she considered for a split second to retract all the things she said to him only a few short months ago. As she stood staring at him in disbelief, she realized what an enormous void his leaving had left behind. All she felt lately was sadness.

A kind of sadness that brought chaos to her heart, and wretched tears to her eyes. She was angry at Adam. She was enraged by the destruction he would inexorably bring into their lives, had she chosen a life with Mark.

"Mark?" She whispered throatily as she held on to her front door, afraid that if she let go, she might lose her balance, and fall to her knees.

"Holly …"

Holly could not mistake a gentle shudder in his almost crackling voice.

"Five minutes, Holly, just five minutes please?" Mark desperately pleaded as he stood staring at her. She seemed happier, almost as though an enormous mountain had been lifted off her shoulders. Her eyes still carried the traces of sadness he had seen not too long ago, but she was no longer as pale as she was when he saw her before he left. His own heart had broken out into a gallop, and he prayed desperately that she would let him in.

Holly stepped slightly to the side when she made way from Mark to enter. When he brushed past her, she was at once reminded of his wonderful musky scent.

She closed the front door and made her way into her living room where she sat down on a chair, before she pointed to a couch in front of her, inviting Mark to take a seat. "You look good, Mark."

"Thanks Holly, so do you."

She smiled sadly before she began fidgeting with her hands. "When did you get back?"

"Only a few minutes ago, hence the uniform." A smile formed around his mouth as he fixed a gaze on her.

"Well, it suits you …"

"Thanks, so listen, Holly, I was there for two months, as you know, and, it's just that, the more I think about it, the more I think there's something you're not telling me. I had so much time to think, and none of this, us, you and me, none of it makes sense to me. I know you said you don't love me, but Holly, I don't believe you?"

"Mar …"

"No Holly, let me finish ..." He interrupted her, determined to have his say after weeks of rehearsing that same conversation in his head.

"I love you, Holly. I do. These two months just made me realize it more. I know you love me. I know, I know, I know you do. I don't know what's going on with you, but if there is one thing I do know, it's that you love me. I don't know why you felt that you had to lie to me, but I don't believe you, Holly."

Holly bowed her head before a familiar, agonizing lump in her throat threatened to silence her.

Mark got up from the couch and knelt before her. He took her trembling hands into his, and softly kissed them, "Holly, we had so many plans. We had dreams. I don't want to let go, and I don't want to lose you. I love you."

A tear rolled desolately down her cheek, and when she looked into his eyes, she could not ignore the desperation in his eyes.

"If you tell me now, right here ..." He paused, desperate to escape the gruffness he could hear in his own voice. "Tell me again that you don't love me, Holly?"

Holly gazed into his murky green eyes. She felt a shudder make its way through her entire body. Her legs began to shake as fiercely as her hands were while staring into the eyes that were begging her for the truth. Mark Quinn was on his knees as though he was clinging to her for dear life.

"Mark …"

"No Holly, I don't want to hear any lies. Just tell me. Tell me what your heart wants. Just tell me."

"My heart does not agree with my mind, Mark. I love you, I do!" She pushed him out of her way and quickly rose to her feet. Mark stood up and stared at her as she brushed past him. She turned around to face him, before she took his face in her hands.

"I love you, Mark. But, I can't do this. I don't want to do this. I don't want to see you ever again!" She yelled out at the top of her voice when she realized she was only moments away from falling apart.

"That makes no sense, Holly!" He grew increasingly frustrated by Holly's odd behavior.

"Nothing makes sense anymore, Mark. Nothing is at it seems or should be!" She fell to her knees, and buried her face in her hands. Again, Mark knelt before her, and took her hands into his.

"Tell me, Holly? I don't understand?"

"I can't ..."

"Then marry me, Holly. Let's get married!"

She freed her hands from his tightening grip and folded them firmly around her waist. "I can never marry you, Mark. Never!"

"Then Holly, you will never see me again, because none of this makes any sense to me. Nothing is right here. You can't give me a sensible answer, and I don't know what's going on?"

Mark got up and offered her a hand. When he helped her to her feet, he turned away from her, and made his way back to the front door. He was sure that a dagger had been plunged into him, and was slowly torturing and killing his soul. He did not want to leave. He did not want to walk away from Holly, but it was the only option she had given him.

As he reached the front door, he turned back to her one last time, "This hurts, Holly. Seeing you drift further away from me just crushes my soul. I want to hold you, and love you, and build a life with you, but if this is what you want …"

While Holly stood listening to him, she realized that he was a broken man. She had broken him, just as Adam had broken her. She stared at him, and knew at that very moment that she could never walk away from Mark. Despite their future, and despite her fate, she loved Mark, and she was willing to risk it all for her moment with him.

"Mark …" She ran up to him and took his hands into hers, "Listen to me. Don't say anything, just listen. Two years from now, you find my body on a floor in our bedroom. I saw you come in, and I can still remember the look on your face …"

Holly knew that she would make no sense to Mark, but she owed it to him and to herself to try and explain the cruel twists life was about to hand them.

Mark glared skeptically at her, and when he opened his mouth, she placed her index finger firmly against it, "I know this sounds crazy, Mark. I know, you don't have to look at me like that. I know how it sounds. But, you must at least consider, even just open your mind a little to what I am saying, okay?"

"Holly, you are scaring me?"

THE BOOKSTORE SERIES
A Crinkle in Time – Book 2

"I am alone in our apartment. It's late. I found out I was pregnant earlier that day, and called you. I wanted you to come home to tell you, but you had already agreed to work a double shift. Adam didn't pitch for work at District 61. You work for District 59." Holly paused and swallowed back on a brand-new lump, only this time, it was a lump she could somewhat control, "I was waiting up for you when Adam showed up claiming to be looking for you. He, it all just went so crazy after that. Everything happened so fast, but he beat me, raped me, and left me for dead after he stabbed me with one of our own kitchen knives."

"Holly?" Mark felt his own legs grow weak underneath him. He stumbled as he moved closer to her and grabbed onto the wall next to her.

"You found me only minutes later, Mark. You found me lying in a pool of my own blood. It was awful. It was horrible. I didn't want you to find me like that. I don't want you to find me like that someday, Mark. Don't you understand? There was blood everywhere, I can still smell it. I can still smell the tobacco and whiskey on his breath …"

Mark slowly made his way back into the living room, and collapsed onto a couch, overcome with shock and not at all convinced that Holly was sane. He sat up straight and buried his head in his hands.

Holly sat down beside him, and gently rubbed his back.

"Holly, maybe it was just a dream? A very bad dream …"

"Mark, I thought it was a dream. Coming back, waking up in August 2002. I thought that I was dreaming when I saw my mother again, the day before she was supposed to die. We weren't at the hospital by accident, Mark. I knew she was going to die, but I thought I could save her." Holly quickly wiped the tears that were oozing from her eyes,

"You see, in this whole other world, she died at home, in her bed, and in her sleep. I found her the next morning. This time I thought, I just thought that if I could get her to a doctor, she would be fine. And it seemed she would be fine, but, she wasn't, and it turns out, she was never my one more last chance."

Mark nodded his head as he stared out in front of him. "Holly, you can't know for sure what the future holds. Nobody can accurately predict the future. Nobody knows, Holly? Nobody can tell you about what you have not yet lived …"

"But, I have Mark, I have lived it. I lived every single moment of it."

Alice VL

"Holly, you can't turn your back on me just because you think something bad might happen? Adam would never do that? I mean, I know you don't like him, but Adam? We're talking about Adam, he could never do that?"

"He does, Mark, and I wish with my whole heart that you believed me ..."

"I mean, Holly. I can tell that you believe it. I know you believe that it was all real and that somehow, you had a premonition, but, I just can't accept that we can predict our future. I can't for the life of me even begin to wrap my head around this?"

Holly lowered her head when she realized that she could not convince Mark. "It was not a premonition, Mark. It was real. I lived it! You are not listening to me!" Holly yelled out and grew increasingly frustrated with Mark, "I met Sarah Kingsley from Fine Books. She wrote a book, A Moment in Time based on her own experiences which were similar to mine. Please, won't you just hear her out and speak to her and her husband, Daniel?"

Mark rose to his feet and walked over to the window. Holly followed him, and gently placed her hand on his shoulder. "I love you, Mark. And if there is any way that you can even consider that what I am telling you is the truth, then I don't want to lose you. You believing me might be all that saves me, and we might then be together. Maybe we can alter little things to change my fate and the fate of our child?"

Mark turned around and held her firmly against him, "Give me time, Holly, okay? Maybe later on I'll consider meeting your friends, just give me some time to process all of this."

"Okay, just promise me you will try?" Holly leaned in closer to him until her lips touched his. Again, she felt a jolt run down her spine, and when he pressed her against him, Holly knew that she could never walk away from Mark, even though her life depended on it.

She loved Mark with all that was within her. She already knew what their future had in store for them, but she was ready to fight destiny and alter their course, whether or not Mark believed her. She remembered what Sarah had told her about faith, and for the first time since her return to that moment in time, Holly wanted to have faith in Mark.

Mark kissed her fiercely, and when he retreated slightly, he smiled from ear to ear.

"Just promise me one thing, Mark, that you'll see the

signs. Just swear to me that you will pay attention of everything around you on February 12th, 2005?"

"That's two years to the day? I can do that, Holly, but Adam? Adam does not have a murderous bone in his body?"

"Yeah, that's what makes him so dangerous. The world can't see it, and neither did I. February 12th, 2005, okay?"

He kissed her again and held her tightly in his arms. "I won't let anything happen to you, Holly. I love you."

PART NINE

Holly had just made her way into her studio, when she heard an intruding knock on her front door. She was at once agitated by the intended interruption early that Friday morning, but she was excited to find Mark standing there.

"Hi, aren't you supposed to be at work?" Holly smiled, before she placed her arms around him.

"I have a few days off, but the reason I'm here ..." He took both her hands into his, and when he smiled excitedly at her, Holly could sense that enthusiasm for some unknown reason to her, had welled up inside of him.

"Come with me quickly!" He gently tugged at her.

"Where to?"

"It's a surprise, please!"

"Alright, let me just get my bag and lock up." Holly ran back into the studio and grabbed her bag. When she reached the front door, Mark was nowhere to be seen, and when she peered out, she noticed him already in the pick-up, anxiously waiting for her. She locked her front door and hurriedly made her way over to him, before she swiftly slid into the passenger seat.

Mark winked at her before he pulled out of her driveway. They drove in silence for a few moments, and when he turned into town, Holly knew instinctively where they were heading.

She could at once remember the day as though it had happened only days before. He had, without her knowledge, put an offer in on an apartment in the center of town, one she was eventually murdered in.

The hairs on her neck began to rise, as an eerie quiver slowly made its way down her spine. She could feel the blood drain from her face as fear entirely immersed her.

When they pulled up to the apartment building, she made a heroic effort to remain as composed and unruffled as she possible could. Mark hurried over to the passenger seat, and opened the car door for her. He smiled excitedly when he took her hand. Holly reluctantly followed him into what was once their dream apartment.

When they reached the elevator, she squeezed his hands

just as she realized hers had turned ice cold.

Holly had no idea of how to cope with the emotions that were beginning to wholly overpower her. In the grip of a silent panic, her heart was racing wildly, and it felt as though her body was on fire.

She could hear a shrill scream from deep inside of her, but thankfully, nothing came out of her mouth. Panic had entered the very core of her. She could feel it grow inside of her like an unstoppable avalanche in the pit of her stomach. She could not concentrate on much else as she mechanically took one step after another.

She followed Mark into the elevator, and forced a smile as she listened to the many arguments between her heart and her mind. When they finally reached the apartment, Mark softly knocked on the door before a well-dressed, attractive woman opened.

"You must be Mark Quinn?"

"Yes …" Mark shook her hand before he turned to Holly,

"This is Holly …"

The woman extended a welcoming hand to Holly, and

smiled warmly at her, "I am Claire Swanson of Claire Swanson Realty …"

Holly frowned when she heard her last name, "I know you. You sold my mother's house? Are you by any chance related to Sarah Kingsley?"

"I sold your mother's house? You know Sarah? Yes, she's my youngest sister?"

"I mean, you'll probably sell my mother's house someday. I've heard so much about you from Sarah. It is so nice to finally meet you, Claire …"

"Any friend of Sè, is a friend of the family. Please, come inside, and allow me to show you this gem of a property."

Holly had managed to cast her fears aside for only a moment, as she followed Claire inside.

When they walked in, she could at once detect the excitement in Mark's voice again, "Isn't this great?"

He impatiently pulled her into the entrance hall, and slowly, they made their way from room to room. Claire and Mark were so caught up in the exhilaration of walking through the apartment, that Holly did not have the heart to tell him about the events that once took place in Mark's dream home.

When they reached the main bedroom, Holly stood motionlessly in the doorway, her eyes fixated in horror on the exact spot where she let out her final breath.

As though it was all playing out right in front of her, she began to quiver violently. It was almost as though she was transported back to the night of the horrific events. She could still see the blood around her, and she could still smell the stale blood hanging in the air.

She felt the tension grow in every part of her body, from her face right down to her limbs as she replayed Adam's brutal assault on her. Her breathing became more rapid as her heart began to thrash violently in her chest.

She could remember every detail from that night as though it was on fast forward. She wanted her thoughts to slow down just enough to allow her to take in a breath of fresh ear.

When the room began spinning, Holly hurriedly turned away, and ran from the apartment. She ran as fast as her legs could carry her down the stairs until she had finally reached the ground floor.

She could not bear one minute longer in that apartment, and she could not stand to walk through the building even one more time. When she reached Mark's pick-up, she finally allowed her tears to flow freely.

Mark caught up to her instantly, disoriented and afraid. He could in no way at all, fathom why she had run so manically from the apartment, almost as though something was chasing her.

He saw her hunched over at the pick-up, and at once, he felt terror make its way into his heart. He nervously walked over to her, before he knelt in front of her. "Holly?"

Holly was at once startled when she heard the panic in his voice. "I can't go in there, I can't …"

"Why not? What happened?"

Before Holly could respond, Claire quickly made her way over to them. "We can talk in my office later. I have another meeting, but whenever you're ready?" Claire was at once unnerved by Holly's odd behavior, and in no way at all, intended to intrude on whatever it was that had upset her so tremendously.

"Thanks Claire. I'll call you later?" Mark quickly shook her hand before she found her way back to her own car. Holly had climbed into the passenger seat of the pick-up, and hastily wiped the tears from her eyes.

When Mark climbed into the driver's seat, he turned to face her, "Holly, you're scaring me?"

Holly grabbed his hands, and squeezed them while the dread of that night was still fresh on her mind, "This is where it happens, Mark."

"What happens, Holly? What?"

"This is where I die, where Adam comes in and …" She was once again silenced by a familiar, yet uninvited bulge in her throat. "Mark! Listen to me! This is where you find me in a pool of my own blood! This is where our child dies! I know you don't believe me, but I have no reason to lie!" Holly raised her voice as frustration began to mount inside of her, "And you, Mark, you've already made an offer on this place! And next, you're going to tell me to sell my mother's house, and use the money to convert the loft into a studio for me! Anything sound familiar to you?"

Mark frowned but shrugged off her supposed prediction as a coincidence, "Come on, Holly, of course I put an offer in. The price is well under market value, and it's all I can afford on my salary. I would think you'd want to sell your mother's house?"

"No Mark, I don't. I did once before, and I've regretted it ever since. And you know what? Claire! Claire sold my mother's house in another time!"

"I just don't understand you, Holly?"

"You don't have to understand me, Mark. Just believe me! And, Mark, just love me enough to listen to me!" Holly shouted again, before she burst out crying one more time. Mark placed his arms around her, and gently kissed her forehead.

As though a light bulb began to flicker in Holly's mind, she withdrew from Mark, and looked him firmly in the eye, "I think this is it, Mark?"

"This is what?"

"I think this is the answer. This is how I stop it!"

"I have no clue what you're saying, Holly."

"If we don't get this apartment, I can't be murdered there. It will change the sequence of events. It will change the course of our lives, and it will alter my fate. It has to. I won't die.

We can be together, and I won't die."

Mark shook his head before he let out a frustrating sigh.

"Mark listen to me! This is how we do it! We don't get this apartment, and we don't move out of my mother's house. We live there, you and I?"

"Holly, I can't move in with you. You're supposed to move in with me?"

"I don't care, Mark. I want to keep my mother's house and live there, and, if you love me as you say you do, you will let me. You will do this one thing for me even if it goes against every single principal of yours ..."

Mark remained silent for what felt like an eternity to Holly. She grew progressively nervous, and when she noticed the distant look in his eyes, she was afraid of what Mark might say.

"Alright Holly. For now. Just for the time being. Until, until this, whatever it is that you're going through, blows over. When is this supposed to happen again?"

"February 12th, 2005."

"Right, but after that, I never want to hear about this

again. Can we agree on that? No more talk about dying and murder and fate and destiny. Nothing. Alright?"

Holly nodded before she flung her arms around him, and held him lovingly against her. "I love you, Mark ..."

"I love you too, Holly, and if you can't see that now, you never will."

She kissed him gently and smiled tenderly at the only man she knew, she could ever love.

When Mark dropped her off at home, she was eager to pay a visit to Sarah at Fine Books. She wanted to tell Sarah how she had avoided the apartment, and by doing so, she had in all likelihood, dodged her own murder.

Alice VL

When she walked through the large, wooden doors of Fine Books, she was instantly relieved that Sarah was alone behind the counter.

"Sarah!" She shouted out as she hurriedly walked over to her. Sarah smiled when she saw Holly, and for the first time since she had met her, she could see a change in Holly's mood.

"You're chirpy today! What happened?" Sarah quickly made her way around to Holly, eager to hear what had made her so happy, and what was responsible for the sudden change in her demeanor.

"Mark and I, we've sort of worked things out. He took me to the apartment today, and actually, your sister Claire showed it to us."

"Oh?" Sarah frowned while listening to Holly ramble on almost incoherently.

"Anyways, I convinced Mark that we should stay at my mother's house!"

"Okay? Is that why you are so happy?" Sarah was confused and desperately tried to make sense of what Holly was saying.

"Yes!"

"Okay? I don't get it?"

"Don't you see, Sarah? If we don't get the apartment, Adam can't murder me there! If I don't live there, I can't be assaulted there …"

Sarah felt a sudden tremor run through the very core of her. She was not quite sure that a change of venue would in fact, alter her fate. The fact that Holly and Mark would not move into the apartment where she is destined to be assaulted someday, did not quite convince Sarah that her fate had been altered.

She did not want to frighten Holly any more than she had been the last few months, and decided against voicing her concerns to Holly. Sarah knew she had to do something to intervene, yet, she had no idea of what to do next.

"Sarah? Why are you frowning?"

"Oh sorry! I'm just trying to absorb everything …"

"Now I can marry Mark! I think I got it right, Sarah. I think I can now begin with my one more last chance, my do-over?" She excitedly placed her arms around Sarah and hugged her animatedly.

THE BOOKSTORE SERIES
A Crinkle in Time – Book 2

When Holly walked out, Sarah knew without a doubt that Holly's fate had not yet been altered. Into the very central part of her, she had a nagging feeling that nothing had changed.

She was afraid for Holly, and she did not have the heart to tell her of the intense fear that was beginning to haunt her.

She knew that she had to find a way to intervene before that fateful night. Sarah made a decision to complete A Crinkle in Time, and hope that her efforts, and what she would do with the manuscript would ultimately be the answer to altering her destiny, just as it once had Daniel's.

THE BOOKSTORE SERIES
A Crinkle in Time – Book 2

Alice VL

PART TEN

Sarah anxiously unlocked the wooden doors to Fine Books just before the sun was about to rise on the morning of February 12th, 2005. She had barely slept a wink the night before, and could not shake an unsettling feeling that had crept up on her in the days leading up to that morning.

When she did fall asleep, Sarah dreamed that she was trapped in a room, paralyzed, naked and cold. A masked man, carrying a knife would appear in front of her as he came closer and closer to her.

She would awake just as he lunged at her with the knife, leaving her feeling terrified. Her heart hammered with extreme force against her rib cage, making it almost impossible for her to breathe.

When she drifted off to sleep again, she dreamed that she had walked through heavy gates that closed behind her, just as she had entered a graveyard. There were rows and rows of graves, and there were rows and rows of crosses on both sides of her. Sarah was alone in the graveyard and as she looked around her, she noticed a beautiful lilac scarf that was folded around a tombstone.

She quickly walked over to the scarf and when she saw Holly's name imprinted into the boulder, her legs caved in underneath her as she sobbed wretchedly on Holly's grave.

When Sarah woke up from her last dream for the night, she refused to go back to sleep. She got dressed, and quickly kissed Daniel on the cheek before she headed out to Fine Books.

As Sarah drove through the streets of Hazel Creek, almost an hour before the sun was due to rise, she could not control the tears that had begun to roll down her cheeks, and dribble onto her chin.

The world around her turned into a blur as all the sounds around her drowned out and faded into the darkness that had not yet been pierced by the morning sun. Sarah felt as though she was losing her mind, and knew that the most important thing she would ever do that day, would be to save Holly's life.

Holly and Mark were married in a beautiful ceremony that was held at her mother's house on a warm, summer's evening. Sarah was delighted when Holly asked her to be her maid of honor while Cindy happily arranged a bachelorette's party for her the weekend before. Sarah was saddened that Holly was an only child, but Cindy happily stepped in for Danielle to ensure a perfect wedding day.

Claire and Megan joined in with all the preparations for her most beautiful day, leaving Holly to feel as though she had been given a brand-new family. Thomas was emotionally overwhelmed when Holly asked him the night before her wedding if he would walk her down the aisle to which he tearfully, yet, happily agreed.

Just as he did with Sarah, Benjamin built Holly her very own pergola in her garden, and they all worked tirelessly to drape thousands of white roses around it.

Cindy kept the seat next to her in the garden open, and told Holly that when she looked over at that empty chair, she should look closer and see Danielle sitting there.

She assured Holly that there was no time or no universe in between that could keep Danielle from her daughter's wedding. She would be there, Holly just had to have faith.

Mark had moved into Danielle's house the day after the wedding, and although life had returned to normal for both Mark and Holly, Sarah could not escape the nudging feeling that her course had not yet been altered.

On the outside, Sarah made a brilliant effort to conceal her concerns and fears to Holly and to the remainder of the world, but inside, she was waging an on-going warfare with herself.

When Sarah walked into Fine Books, she anxiously ran upstairs, and quickly began working on what was then, an almost completed manuscript. By the following day, Holly's book, A Crinkle in Time would be complete, the ending decided.

Sarah told Daniel the previous night that she wanted to finish it off early and stop by District 59 to give it to Mark. She was desperate for Mark to perhaps, notice the signs should Holly's future be unaltered, or at the very least, be undecided as yet.

She thought back to their unique friendship, one that began with Passage of Time, and the events that brought her to Fine Books. She had grown increasingly protective of Holly, and she valued a friendship that had begun to flourish between them.

Excitement welled up inside of her when she remembered Holly once telling her how she would find out she was pregnant on that very day. It would also be the day, according to Holly, they had met for the very first time.

Once Sarah typed out the last page of the incomplete manuscript, she quickly printed it out, and placed it into a folder. She ran downstairs and waited anxiously for Cindy to stand in for her while she rushed out to find Mark at the fire station.

When Sarah heard the chiming of the doorbell, she was at once unsettled and unprepared to find Holly walk in. "Holly?"

"Hi Sarah, I actually made my doctor's appointment earlier. I am so excited knowing what I know! I just don't think I can wait till this afternoon!"

Sarah smiled broadly before she took Holly's hands into hers. "I am so happy for you, Holly, what time is your appointment?"

"It's in ten minutes. I just, well, today is the day I walked in here for the very first time. And to think, this same night, it was all over for me ... once." She whispered sadly as she glanced around the bookstore.

"I am just so glad it's over, Sarah! I am so glad that it's a part of my life that is truly over."

"Me too, Holly. You just gotto have faith in Adelaine Alandrali. So, listen, I have some errands to run this morning, do you want me to come over tonight?" She paused, as she did her best to remain composed, but desperate for Holly not to be alone that night.

"I mean, do you want the four of us to do something tonight? Maybe celebrate?"

"No, but thank you, Sarah! I really just want to give Mark the news tonight when we're alone. I am planning a dinner, and when he comes home, hopefully, I can surprise him! I must just remember to ask him early not to work a double shift."

Sarah once again felt a quiver run down her spine. "Alright, but please, Holly, call me if you need me, okay?"

"Everything's fine, Sarah. I'll be fine! Tomorrow, we'll laugh about all of this, and we can finally add an ending to A Crinkle in Time. I am so excited about that!"

"It still doesn't change the fact that Adam is a murderer, Holly?" Sarah's bitter words slipped out before she could stop them.

"If he doesn't commit a murder, he isn't one, right?"

"I suppose …"

Before Holly could respond, Cindy walked in, pleased to see Holly. "Hello lovey! You look pretty!"

"Thank you, Cindy …" She ran up to Cindy and flung her arms around her. Cindy frowned as she gazed over at Sarah.

"Today she finds out she's having a baby, remember?"

"Oh, that's right! Congratulations, Holly!"

"Thank you, Cindy."

Holly turned back to Sarah, before she lifted her hand to wave, "So, I'll speak to you later?"

"Be careful, Holly!" Sarah shouted out before Holly walked out of Fine Books.

"Mommy, something doesn't feel right? I have such a bad, bad feeling. I don't think it's over …"

"Did you warn Holly?"

"No, she is so sure that she's altered her fate. I don't have the heart to tell her, especially today …"

"We must do something?"

Alice VL

"I sort of invited myself over to her house tonight, but she made it clear she's planning a surprise for Mark, and that they want to be alone?"

"Why don't you and Daniel go around anyways?"

Sarah stood motionlessly as a million thoughts and a gazillion ideas flooded her mind. "I am taking the manuscript to Mark at the fire house. I am going to beg him to read it, and then I am going to demand he pays attention to the signs. That's all I can do other than sit outside her house in my car, which I will do if it comes to that!"

"Why don't you ask Daniel to take the manuscript to Mark? It will sound better coming from Daniel seeing as he has gone through all of this?"

Sarah's eyes widened before she smiled from ear to ear, "Mother, you are brilliant!"

Sarah turned, around and hurriedly picked up her mobile phone, before she frantically dialed Daniel. "Danny?"

"Hey Sè, what's up?"

"Can you pop in quickly please?"

"Sure, I am just around the corner."

"Thank you!" Sarah ended the call and ran up to the large wooden doors of Fine Books.

When the door opened, she shoved the manuscript into his hands.

"Boy, this sure feels like de ja vu?" Sarah giggled, before she quickly kissed Daniel on the cheek.

"What must I do with this?" He sighed and frowned all at the same time.

"I need you to go and see Mark at the fire house. You've been through this Daniel. You know all about signs. I need you to ask him to read this manuscript. It contains the events of today that have not yet happened, and then you ask him to see the signs. Tell him about tonight, tell him about Adam. Even if it sounds crazy tell him, Daniel. Even if he doesn't believe you, you must make him believe everything you say! You must tell him about the ship and my manuscript. You must tell him, Danny."

"He'll think I'm nuts!"

"Even so, Danny. She dies tonight. And so does her child. You need to make him understand that she dies tonight, and you can start by telling him that Adam will call in sick, and he will volunteer a double shift, okay? Tell him that Holly is going to call him, and ask him to come home early. Tell him that she will say that she wants dinner with him. Tell him that she wants to tell him about the baby, but that he had already agreed to a double shift because Adam called in sick. After that, when it happens, he'll see the signs. I know he will."

"Can't we just go over to their place tonight?"

"I tried that …"

"Okay fine, but if his fire fighter buddies load me up and drop me off at a mental institution, you better come and get me out!"

He placed his arms around her, and gently squeezed her. "I love you, Sè …"

"I love you plenty!" Daniel turned around, and made his way back to his car. He placed the manuscript on the passenger seat, before he drove off in the direction of the fire house.

Alice VL

When Daniel pulled into District 59, he was just in time to catch Mark who was about to start his shift.

"Hey buddy!" Mark called out when he spotted Daniel climbing out his car.

"Glad I caught you before work …"

Mark walked over to Daniel's car, and quickly shook his hand. "What brings you here?"

"Damn, I don't think I'll ever get used to this …" Daniel was lost for words. He had no clue of how to explain the series of events that could quite possible play out before the next morning.

"Are you okay?" Mark frowned when he noticed the tension on Daniel's face. He could barely ignore the strain in his eyes, or how he had begun clenching his jaw.

Daniel reached for the manuscript and handed it over to Mark, "I get this all sounds crazy. I was you once, Mark. I was once on a ship, getting a manuscript just like this one. This is Holly's story, Mark. Sarah needs you to read it. There is no ending yet, and Sarah thinks you might be able to help with that."

"Holly's story? Does Holly know about any of this?"

Alice VL

"She knows about the book, but she thinks she's changed her destiny. Sarah isn't saying that it hasn't changed, she's just asking you to read the manuscript and notice the signs. Be ready for anything that doesn't feel right today, okay? Anything, a feeling, anything, Mark. Just trust me on this." He paused to take in a deep breath when he detected the perplexity in Mark's eyes. "I didn't believe in any of this either, Mark. I didn't want to listen, and I was almost too late. I know better now. So please, do this for Holly, do this for you and do this for your child. Read it and if anything starts making sense to you, you can stop it. Only you can stop all of this. You must. Holly finds out she's pregnant today."

"Holly's pregnant?"

"She's on her way to the doctor as we speak. Congratulations, by the way. You can't say anything to her, do you understand? You cannot tell her you know, and you can't tell her about the manuscript. Read it, it's all in there, just trust this book. Adam is going to call in sick. You're going to volunteer a double shift. While you're working his shift, he will be over at your place … I can't even say it. She will call you about having dinner with her tonight because she wants to tell you about the baby …"

Mark nodded and gazed down at the manuscript in his

hands. He quickly shook Mark's hand before he turned to begin his day.

After Daniel pulled out of the fire station, Mark quickly placed the manuscript on his desk, and grabbed his attendance register. When he met the rest of the crew in the communal area, he quickly got through marking off the attendees and the absentees.

It was just after four in the afternoon when Chief Dowdes from District 61 called Mark, "Quinn, it's Chief Dowdes."

"Good afternoon, sir. What can I do for you?"

"Are you still volunteering double shifts?

"Yes sir."

"Great. Can you clock in after your shift at 59? Weston has called in sick."

"Sure, no problem …" He quickly replaced the handset and when his eyes caught A Crinkle in Time, he nervously glanced at his watch. He had forgotten about Holly's book, and realized it was almost an hour before his shift would end.

He picked up the manuscript, and glanced over the

pages, before he intently began reading her story. He read about how she had found her mother in her bed one morning in August, and how devastated she was when she came across her lifeless body.

He read about how she woke up a day before her mother's death for a second time, and how sure she was that she could save her life. He read about the night a known intruder came into her home, and brutally assaulted her, leaving Mark to find her just as she was about to breathe out her very last breath.

When he reached the last page, he felt shivers run down his spine, as fear began to take a hold of his heart and seize his entire being. He looked up and gazed out in front of him, sure that Holly must have once had a vivid, haunting dream that convinced her it was perhaps, nothing more than what she believed to be a premonition.

There was nothing else to justify what she thought she had lived, and there was no other way to explain what Holly deemed to be true. Time travel did not exist. It was not possible. It made no sense.

He placed the manuscript back on his desk and could not help but feel a quiver rush through him when he read about the double shift he agreed to fill in for Adam.

Before he could reflect further on the discrepancy that was beginning to gnaw at him, their siren rang out to indicate a shift change. Mark grabbed his gear, and rushed out to his car. Without thinking about the book again, he obediently made his way to District 61.

As he was about to walk into the fire station, his mobile phone rang unexpectedly. When he glanced down at the screen, he was pleased to see a picture of Holly come up. "Hello beautiful?"

Mark was instantly relieved to hear Holly's voice,

"Hello handsome ..." Her heart again, broke out into a flutter when he referred to her as beautiful.

"What's up?"

"Nothing much. Are you working late tonight?"

"Yep. District 59 is short-staffed, so I'll be standing in until about 2 am ..."

"Can't you just miss tonight. You've been at work all day, just tonight?"

"I can't, Holly, I've already agreed to the shift. You should have asked earlier …"

"Yeah, I know. I planned to, but time just got away from me. Please wake me when you get home. I want to have dinner with you …"

"Is everything alright?"

He wanted to ask her about the baby, but again, he was convinced that most of what Sarah and Holly wrote about, was nothing more than her overactive imagination following a crushing nightmare she once had. Still, Mark couldn't ignore the panic that slowly began occupying his entire being.

"Everything's fine, I just see so little of you. Wake me, okay?"

"Alright, see you later, angel. I love you …"

"I love you. Be careful."

The moment Mark ended his call with Holly, he could not help but feel as though they had had that very same discussion before. It entirely unnerved him, and when fear began attacking him from the very core of him, he knew that something was not quite right.

Alice VL

Was it the manuscript, or was it something he could never have begun to imagine? He was still ruminating on his phone call with Holly, when the almost deafening siren of District 61 rang out.

They were at once dispatched to an accident scene only two short miles from the fire house. He immediately placed all thoughts of Holly and the manuscript aside, as they rushed to assist the victims of the wreck.

They were able to quite easily resolve the situation, and when Mark climbed back into the fire truck, he was at once reminded of his conversation with Holly, only, it was recorded word for word in her manuscript. He dialed Holly's number, but there was no reply. He was desperate to reach her, and when he turned to the shift captain, he had become visibly shaken, "I have to go home! My wife is in trouble!"

He shouted out at the top of his voice as dread began spreading through his body like ice-cold, liquid metal which turned to hot lava just as quickly, and began flowing mercilessly through his veins.

His legs began to twitch slightly, and his hands were shaking uncontrollably. The shift captain was at once overwhelmed by the sudden palpitation in his voice as Mark stared pleadingly at him. "Then we'll all go!" The fire truck turned on its siren as the entire squad sped down the streets of Hazel Creek, frantic to reach Mark and Holly's home.

Holly had just made herself comfortable in Mark's living room chair, before she turned on the television. She had scarcely found a channel to settle into, when she heard an urgent knock on their front door.

Holly glanced over at her watch, and when she realized it was almost midnight, she was at once baffled by who it could be. She got up from the living room chair, and slowly made her way to the front door.

She peered through the peeping hole but could see nothing but darkness. She slowly opened the door and stepped back in shock, entirely defeated and overpowered by a fear she had known once before. When she saw him standing there, she could clearly smell the alcohol on Adam's breath,

"Is Mark home?"

Holly was at once terrified by his presence, and shouted out at the top of her voice, "Oh, God no!" Holly felt fear rush through her heart, and trap her entire core in its grip.

She was terrified of Adam, and she was at once horrified when it dawned on her, that nothing had changed. Nothing was different, and she was about to relive her horrific ordeal one more time.

Alice VL

"Yeah, yeah, whatever …"

He pushed past her and made his way into the kitchen.

"Adam, I, I know what you're going to do. I am begging you …" She kept the front door open, hopeful that someone might hear the chaos that was about to erupt in her home, on their quiet street.

"Do you? Really?"

"Adam, I am pregnant. Mark is your best friend?"

"Oh, get over yourself, Sarah!" Adam walked over to her, and ran his fingers down her blouse.

"Stop that!" Holly pushed his hands away and retreated slightly. She again noticed a look in Adam's eyes she had never seen before that night, and again, it scared her almost to death.

"Why? You were a slut in college and you are a slut now!" He shouted out as he grabbed her hands into his.

"You are hurting me, Adam!"

"Oh, this is nothing compared to what's waiting for you!"

"I know what's waiting for me, Adam! Don't do this!

Please, don't do this to us?"

Still clutching her hands, he dragged her to her bedroom, and threw her onto the floor. When she hit the floor, she knocked her head on the cold tiles, causing her to lose consciousness almost at once.

Alice VL

THE BOOKSTORE SERIES
A Crinkle in Time – Book 2

Alice VL

A CRINKLE IN TIME

"Holly? Holly?"

Holly desperately tried to open her weighty and drowsy eyes. The world around her was a blur as random images floated aimlessly in front of her. She peered groggily ahead of her, and was instantly relieved to find Mark standing over her.

"Oh no, not again …" She whispered under her breath as she desperately tried to open her eyes.

"Hey honey, how are you feeling?"

"Adam?" Holly shouted out as she gathered up all her strength to sit upright. She felt a sharp pain that began in her belly and echoed throughout her body. She was sure that it was the vicious stab wounds left by Adam after he violently speared her with her own kitchen knife.

"Holly, are you okay?"

"Where is Adam? Where am I?"

Alice VL

"You're in hospital, Hazel Creek Medical Centre, everything's okay, Holly ..."

"Where? Where is Adam?"

Mark sat down next to her on the bed, and gently propped up the pillow behind her. "Don't you remember anything?"

"I mean, he beat me. I fell and hit my head, and I can't remember anything after that. I survived this time?"

"Holly, you were right. I read your manuscript after Daniel brought it by the fire house. Everything was exactly as you said it would be." Mark swallowed back on a curbing, severely bulging lump in his throat while Holly stared suspiciously at him.

"We were just about to go back to the fire station after we were called out to an accident when it hit me. The captain on duty had the entire crew take a drive past our house. I saw the door open and knew, I just knew ..."

Holly took his hands, and tightly squeezed them.

"I got to you just as Adam was about to rape you. The knife was lying next to him, he was planning on stabbing you, Holly. He was going to kill you. He had every intention of slaying you that night, Holly. I have never seen Adam like that before. I would never have believed it if I hadn't seen it for myself. It was like looking at the devil himself …"

Holly swallowed back on her own tears, desperate to keep them from flooding her eyes, "Where is Adam now?"

"He, he's gone. He didn't make it …" Mark lowered his head, before he burst into tears.

"What do you mean?"

"He was my best friend, Holly. And, when I saw what he was doing to you, I thought I was too late. You were laying so still. I thought, I just thought, I thought you were gone."

"Oh no, Mark …"

"I did what I had to do to protect you and our daughter. And the team, the rest of the crew just left me, they let me do what I needed to do, Holly, and I am not sorry. I did what I had to do."

"Our daughter? What do you mean, our daughter?"

"You really don't remember anything from the last seven months?"

Alice VL

"The last seven months? What are you talking about, Mark?" Holly was overcome by shock as she tried to piece together the last seven months. She had no memory of the attack after Adam beat her, and she could remember nothing since then and up to that very moment.

"It's September 17th …"

"It's September? Oh no? That means, oh no. I am sorry, Mark …"

"What are you sorry for, Holly? You have nothing to be sorry for."

"For letting Adam take our child …"

At that very moment, the door to her hospital room opened. When a nurse walked in carrying a baby in her arms, Holly was at once overcome with shock and without reservation, she allowed the tears to flow freely from her eyes.

Mark stood up and took the baby from the nurse's arms. He walked on over to Holly, and placed their daughter on her chest, "Meet your little girl, Holly. You're here in hospital because you gave birth to her …"

Holly cried uncontrollably when she held her tiny little

girl in her arms. Her daughter had survived the attack. She had survived the assault. In her wildest dreams, she never thought she would wake up to a brand-new world where Adam was no longer a fraction of it.

A world where her daughter was real. She could never have imagined that she would wake up to find that she had given birth to the baby she had once lost. They were safe, and Mark saw the signs.

"Sarah was right ..." She whispered as she gently kissed her little girl on the forehead. "I had to have faith that you'd see the signs."

Mark bent down, and kissed Holly, "If Daniel didn't stop by, Holly, I would never have known what the signs were. We owe them everything."

"I just, I have no memory of the last seven months?" Holly whimpered while holding her baby snugly against her.

"Oh Holly, we've had a wonderful seven months. We have never before been as happy as now, and I, I don't mind telling you about it every day for the rest of your life, if that's what you need. We are going to be okay. Our daughter is going to be just fine, and that's all that matters ..."

Alice VL

THE BOOKSTORE SERIES

A Crinkle in Time – Book 2

Holly gazed up at him and Mark couldn't ignore the sudden fear in her eyes, "What's going to happen to you, Mark? I mean, Adam, and what happened that night? What's going to happen to you?"

Mark gently stroked her cheek before he held her hand protectively in his, "Nothing. I was arrested that night, but the entire crew testified that it was self-defense. Nothing, Holly, it's over. They were all witness to Adam's attack on you."

Holly smiled and let out an enormous sigh of relief before she turned back to the little girl in her arms, "We have to think of a name for her? I have a few ideas …" Holly gazed up at Mark, as her tears continued to trickle from the corners of her eyes. "I read the story of The Legend of Adelaine Alandrali. All of this was because of Adelaine and her own heartbreak. She made this happen. It was her magic, Mark, and I kind of feel that it's because of her that we're here, and that we got our one more last chance."

Mark smiled sadly, "Adelaine …"

"Addy." Holly whispered as she traced every inch of her daughter's face with her finger tips.

"I love it, Adelaine Quinn …"

Alice VL

"No, Adelaine Danielle Quinn …"

There was another sudden knock on Holly's door. When Mark opened it, he was ecstatic to find Sarah and Daniel standing there, holding a bunch of balloons and a beautiful flower bouquet.

"She doesn't remember much from the last seven months, so, try not to say too much. I think it's a side effect of this, whatever it is?" Mark made way for Sarah and Daniel to walk in.

"Sarah!" Holly shouted out as Sarah rushed excitedly over to her hospital bed. Sarah placed a book on the bed beside her, before she bent down to survey the little girl laying in Holly's arms.

"Oh Holly, she is so beautiful. She looks just like her daddy, and a little like her grandmother …"

"She sure does …"

"I don't remember much since the attack, Sarah? I don't know why? Mark says that we were happy and looking forward to the baby, but I don't remember much?"

"I lost fourteen years, Holly. Apparently, very good

years." She winked at Daniel who was listening from a distance.

"I have put it down to a side effect. My mother believes that there is always a price to pay for altering our fate, and perhaps, that's the price we've had to pay? I don't mind, I'd take it any day. If you think about it Holly, it's a very small price …"

She hugged Holly before she took her hand and tightly squeezed it. "I can't tell you how thankful I am that you are here, Holly. To think it all could have ended so differently …"

"If it weren't for you and Daniel, it most probably would have. Thank you, Sarah. When did you know? When did you figure it out? When did you realize that nothing was different and that, that nothing had changed?"

"I've always known, Holly. I knew from the moment you said you weren't getting the apartment, I knew that nothing had changed. Mark had to believe you before it could change, just like Daniel once had to believe me."

"You didn't say anything?"

"I didn't want to say anything until we could come up with a plan, and we did. You were so excited to go to the doctor's, and I hadn't seen you as happy in the weeks before that day or actually, since I met you. There was just no point in telling you, Holly."

Sarah gently stroked Adelaine's cheek, "Have you thought of a name for her?"

"We have, Adelaine ..." Sarah was at once surprised, and glanced over at Holly before she hugged her tightly,

"She would be so honored. I bet you she is smiling down on us right now."

When Holly noticed the book lying next to her, she slowly picked it up, and stared questioningly at Sarah. "A Crinkle in Time? We did it?"

"We sure did. That is your story, Holly. I think you will be pleasantly surprised to see how it ended, and how you and I worked together to finish it. Come to think of it, I think we will have to start a book club with all these one more last chances." Sarah let out a faint giggle.

"Do you think it's just us?"

"I don't know, Holly? But, what I do know is that Adelaine found you through The Passage of Time, and I will be surprised if she doesn't find someone else who deserves their one more last chance."

"If it happens again, we'll be right here to guide her through her one more last chance."

"We sure will, Holly, we sure will …"

Mark, Holly and Adelaine … until next time!

THE END